The Creator and the Purpose of Creation

The collected works of Sriram Nagarajan

By Sriram Nagarajan

First edition.

The Creator and the Purpose of Creation

This collected edition contains the complete texts of the following works by Sriram Nagarajan, originally published during 2026:

- Parenting Begins Before Birth: A Guide to Conscious Intent for Expecting Parents (ISBN: 9798248124862)
- The Flower That Never Blossomed: A Journey of Memory, Identity and Love (ISBN: 9798249262266)
- Autonomous Cars and the Clue to God: How Invention Reveals the Invisible Source (ISBN: 9798250772495)
- AI Cannot Surpass Its Creator: A Journey beyond Evolution toward Self Realization (ISBN: 9798249770105)
- Seriously Serious: Ego, Conditioning, and the Collapse of Cordiality (ISBN: 9798250173728)
- The Story That Was Never Told: A Different Story for Every Reader (ISBN: 9798250241700)

First Edition — 2026

ISBN: 9789357868488

Table of Contents

Preface

Every book I have written began as a question — a question that would not rest until it found its voice. Some asked about the beginnings of life, others about the unfinished blossoms of memory and love. Some turned to invention and technology as mirrors of the invisible source, while others confronted the ego, conditioning, and the untold stories that shape our lives. And finally, one asked how we are to live once truth itself has been revealed.

Though each of these works was born as a standalone inquiry, together they form a single thread. They are not fragments but facets of one journey — the search for the Creator and the purpose of creation. This collected edition is not simply a gathering of titles; it is a tapestry woven from questions, reflections, and revelations across time.

I invite you, dear reader, to walk this path not as a spectator but as a participant. Let these pages be mirrors, reflecting your own questions, your own unfinished blossoms, and your own search for the unseen. If these words speak to you, it is because they were never mine alone — they were always waiting for you.

Introduction

The works gathered here are diverse in subject yet united in spirit. They move from the practical to the philosophical, from the personal to the cosmic. At first glance, a book on parenting may seem far removed from a meditation on artificial intelligence or the paradox of seriousness after truth. Yet each is a facet of the same inquiry: What does it mean to live consciously, and why does creation exist at all?

This collected edition is arranged in four parts, each reflecting a stage of the journey:
- **Beginnings and Human Experience** explores the roots of life, memory, and identity.
- **Invention and the Invisible Source** turns to technology as a metaphor for the divine.
- **Ego, Story, and Seriousness** confronts the illusions of conditioning and the untold narratives that shape us.
- **The Final Act** asks how we live authentically once truth has been revealed.

Together, these parts form a philosophical odyssey. You may read them in sequence, or you may choose the book that speaks most directly to your present questions. Either way, the journey is yours — and the answers you discover will always lead back to yourself.

Reader's Guide

This collected edition invites you to enter from many doors. Each book speaks to a different dimension of human experience, and you may begin wherever your questions lead you:

- **For parents and families**

  Parenting Begins Before Birth explores how conscious intent shapes life even before birth.

- **For seekers of memory and identity**

  The Flower That Never Blossomed meditates on love, loss, and the unfinished blossoms of memory.

- **For technologists and inventors**

  Autonomous Cars and the Clue to God and AI Cannot Surpass Its Creator use invention and artificial intelligence as mirrors of the divine.

- **For those wrestling with ego and conditioning**

  Seriously Serious examines how ego and social conditioning collapse cordiality, and how seriousness can be reclaimed as authenticity.

- **For storytellers and seekers of hidden narratives**

  The Story That Was Never Told invites each reader to discover their own untold story.

- **For those ready to face truth directly**

  The Art of Acting Seriously – After Knowing the TRUTH asks how we live authentically once illusions have fallen away.

Part I: Beginnings and Human Experience

Introduction to Part I

Every journey begins with origins. Before invention, before ego, before truth, there is life itself — fragile, mysterious, and unfolding. In this part, we explore the beginnings of human experience: how consciousness is shaped even before birth, and how memory and identity carry blossoms that sometimes never open. These works remind us that creation is not only cosmic but deeply personal, rooted in the intimate stories of family, love, and loss.

Parenting Begins Before Birth

A Guide to Conscious Intent for Expecting Parents

Contents

CHAPTER 1 — The Intent: Why Do We Choose to Become Parents?

Parenting does not begin when a baby is born.

It begins long before that—at the moment a couple decides to bring a new life into their world.

What often gets overlooked is that the foundation of parenting is intent. The clarity behind why parents want a child shapes how they will raise that child. Without consciously realizing it, this intent becomes the invisible compass guiding every decision that follows.

This chapter explores that inner foundation—why we choose parenthood, what conditioning we carry into it, and how the child's own inherent nature meets the parents' intent to begin the lifelong dance of upbringing.

1.1 Understanding the "Why" of Becoming Parents

For many people, starting a family is not a deeply reflected choice—it is an inherited pattern:

- "Everyone eventually has children."
- "It's what a married couple should do."
- "Our parents expect grandchildren."
- "Society considers it a milestone."

These reasons may be true, but they lack personal awareness.

A few couples take a more conscious path:

- "We want to nurture a life."
- "We want a family of our own."
- "We want to experience unconditional love."
- "We want to provide a better environment than we had."
- "We want to shape a human being with values and purpose."

Neither path is right or wrong — but clarity is important.

When challenges arise, it is **intent** that determines how parents respond, support each other, and stay engaged.

A child deserves parents who have thought about *why* they are embarking on this journey.

1.2 Parents Enter Parenthood with Conditioning — Not a Blank Slate

Every expecting parent carries a lifetime of experiences, values, fears, and beliefs. These form a template, often invisible, that influences parenting even before the child arrives.

This conditioning includes:

- What parents think is good or bad
- Ideas about discipline, freedom, success, and failure
- Attitudes about love, responsibility, and respect
- Fears from childhood
- Emotional patterns
- Cultural expectations
- Unfulfilled dreams or regrets

This conditioning quietly shapes how parents will respond to:

- crying
- dependence
- exploration
- risk-taking
- mistakes
- emotional expression

Often, without intending to, parents try to give their child:

- what they wish they received
- what they missed
- or what they wanted to become but couldn't

This is not unhealthy — unless it is unconscious.

Awareness of one's own conditioning is the first step toward mindful parenting.

1.3 The New-born's conditioning: Genes Carry Their Own Blueprint

While parents bring in years of conditioning, the new-born enters life with almost none — yet not entirely empty.

A baby's biological makeup carries inherent tendencies:

- natural temperament
- sensitivity levels
- emotional reactivity
- basic preferences
- energy patterns
- early likes and dislikes

That is why some babies:

- smile easily
- are naturally observant
- are sensitive to sound
- sleep lightly
- are instinctively calm
- get easily overstimulated

These tendencies are not taught — they are *inherited signatures* coded in the genes.

This is the baby's starting conditioning, not their final identity.

Over time, environment and parenting interact with these traits to shape a unique individual.

1.4 Do Babies Have an Intent of Their Own?

We cannot say with certainty whether infants have a conscious intent, but their behavioural patterns show hints of natural direction:

- some gravitate toward exploration
- some seek comfort and closeness
- some show early interest in rhythm, movement, or faces
- some display early independence or sensitivity

These subtle tendencies are like the first strokes on a blank canvas.

As the child grows and the intellect matures, they begin forming their own:

- preferences
- choices
- ambitions

- ways of thinking
- sense of identity

But in the early years, their world is a reflection of their parents.

1.5 How Parental Intent Meets the Baby's Inherent Nature

Parenting is the blending of two forces:

1. **Parents' Intent** — how they want to raise their child
2. **Child's Genetic Blueprint** — how the child naturally is

In the early years, the parents' environment, time, attention, and emotional presence strongly influence the child's life direction.

Parents shape:

- emotional security
- early habits
- thought patterns
- sense of safety
- self-esteem
- early worldview

As the child's intellect grows, they slowly begin shaping themselves.

But the earliest and deepest layers belong to the parents.

This is why the intent of parents must be conscious, not automatic.

1.6 The Power of a Clear Parenting Intent

Having clear intent gives direction to decisions like:

- How much time can we truly give the child?
- What type of environment do we want to create?
- What values matter most to us?
- What fears or insecurities from our past should not pass on?

- What dreams of ours should not become burdens for the child?
- How will we support each other as partners?

Without clarity, parenting becomes reactive.

With clarity, parenting becomes purposeful.

A child does not need perfect parents.

They need **aware parents**.

1.7 Reflection for Expecting Parents

Questions to Ask Before Becoming Parents

1. Why do we truly want a child?
2. What parts of our upbringing do we consciously want to repeat?
3. What parts do we want to change?
4. What are our fears about parenting?
5. How engaged and available can we realistically be?
6. What kind of environment do we dream of giving our child?

This reflection cultivates awareness — the core of mindful parenting.

Chapter 1 Summary

- Parenting begins with intent, not birth.
- Parents carry conditioning from their past.
- Babies bring genetic tendencies of their own.
- Parenting is the merging of parental intent and the child's inherent nature.
- Awareness of one's intent sets the tone for the entire parenting journey.

Chapter 1 – Additions

A. Real-Life Stories & Scenarios

Story 1: The Unconscious Path — Meera & Suresh

Meera and Suresh had been married for four years when relatives began asking, "So… when's the good news?"

With each festival gathering, the pressure grew. They finally decided, "Maybe we should start trying. Everyone our age is having kids."

When their daughter arrived, they loved her deeply but soon realised something:

They had never discussed their parenting values.

Meera believed children must be nourished gently, never scolded.

Suresh believed discipline is the foundation of success.

She wanted to breastfeed exclusively.

He wanted a predictable routine above all.

Their arguments were not about the baby.

They were about **their conditioning**.

Six months later, they sat down and asked the question they skipped at the beginning:

"Why did we choose to become parents? And what kind of parents do we want to be?"

That conversation transformed their parenting journey — not into perfection, but into awareness.

Story 2: The Conscious Path — Arun & Kavya

Arun and Kavya spent a week on a short trip before planning for a baby. On one evening walk, Kavya asked, "What kind of environment do you want our child to grow up in?"

They spoke for hours.

They shared what they loved about their childhoods.

They admitted what they feared passing down.

They listed values they wanted to embody — not enforce.

Their son was born two years later, and parenting was still challenging — nights were sleepless, emotions ran high — but they had a shared foundation to fall back on. Their disagreements never became battles, because their **intent** was aligned.

Their clarity didn't make them perfect.

It made them prepared.

Story 3: The Baby With a Distinct Nature — Little Isha

From birth, Isha was different from her older brother.

Where he was calm and observant, she was expressive and easily frustrated.

Where he slept long hours, she woke frequently.

Where he responded to touch, she responded to rhythm and sound.

Her parents initially tried the same parenting approach for both.

But gradually they recognised something important:

Isha had her own inherent nature, independent of their parenting style.

Her mother often said, "We didn't teach her to be this way. She came with it."

And she was right.

Understanding this helped them adjust expectations, offer personalised responses, and appreciate that each child's genetic signature brings its own unique flavour to life.

B. Illustrations

1. Parents' conditioning vs. Child's Genetic Blueprint

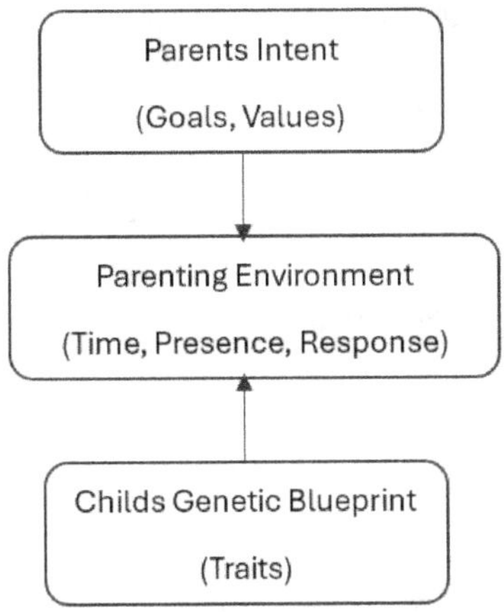

Interpretation:

Parent intent flows downward into their behaviour, while the baby's inherent traits flow upward. Parenting is the meeting point of these two forces.

2. The Three Layers of a Child's Early Identity

Layer 1 (Core): Genetic Tendencies

Layer 2 (Middle): Early Environment from Parents

Layer 3 (Outer): Developing Intellect & Choices

A child begins with **inherent tendencies**, shaped early by **parental environment**, and later forms **their own identity** as intellect matures.

3. The Intent Triangle for Expecting Parents

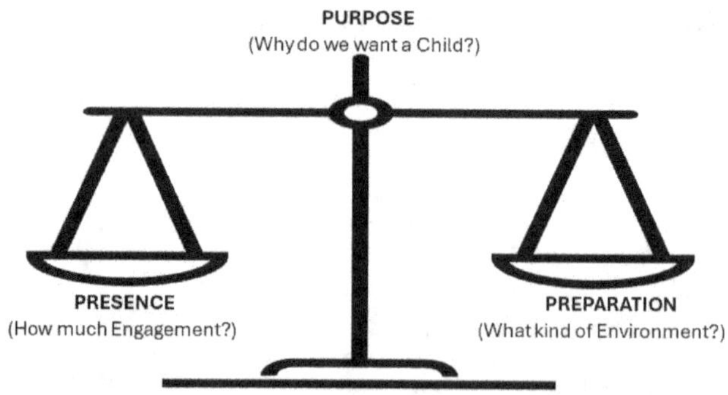

Balanced parenting is where all three meet.

C. Reflection Worksheet for Expecting Parents

1. Self-Reflection Questions

A. Understanding Intent

1. Why do we want to become parents?
2. Are we choosing this consciously or due to social pressure?
3. What excites us about parenting?
4. What scares us about parenting?

B. Evaluating Personal Conditioning

5. What parts of my childhood do I want to pass on?
6. What parts do I want to avoid repeating?
7. What beliefs about discipline and freedom do I carry?
8. How do I express stress? How might that affect our child?

C. Understanding Our Capacity

9. How much time can we genuinely give our child in the early years?
10. Are we prepared for emotional and lifestyle changes?
11. How do we plan to support each other?
12. How will we handle disagreements?

2. Couple Discussion Prompts

- "What values matter most to us as a family?"
- "How will we divide responsibilities when the baby arrives?"
- "What is our philosophy on nurturing vs discipline?"
- "How will we protect our child from our unresolved fears?"

These prompts deepen mutual understanding.

3. Intent Statement (Activity)

Our intent as parents is to create a loving, aware, supportive environment where our child can grow in alignment with their own nature, not our unfulfilled desires.

You can personalise it.

4. Journaling Exercise

Write a one-page letter to your future child describing:

- what kind of parent you hope to be
- what kind of environment you dream of giving
- what values you promise to uphold
- what fears you want to overcome

This becomes a powerful emotional foundation.

CHAPTER 2 — How Parents Create Intent

In the previous chapter, we explored **why intent matters** before a child enters the world. Intent is the seed from which parenting grows. But the natural question that follows is:

How does one create intent?

Is it just a thought?

A desire?

A dream?

A repeated affirmation?

Or something deeper?

Intent is more than all of these.

Intent is **the direction of your inner compass** — the force that guides you even when you are uncertain about how the journey will unfold.

This chapter explores how parents can form a clear, flexible, and shared intent before beginning their parenting journey.

2.1 What Exactly Is Intent?

Intent is not simply:

- an idea
- a wish
- a passing emotion
- a dream
- a plan
- a verbal statement

Intent is a **deep inner clarity** about what you want to create.

It carries a conviction that is not shaken by fear or doubt.

Intent says:

"This is the direction I choose, even if the path is unknown."

Intent is the bridge between desire and reality.

You don't know *how* it will happen — you only know *why* it matters to you.

Parents often struggle here because life has already shown them:

- Some desires come true
- Some remain unfulfilled
- Some never materialize
- Some surprise us
- Some change over time

So when they hear the phrase "create intent," it triggers old memories of success and failure.

And yet, something inside still tells them:

"Intent is necessary. Without intent, nothing begins."

This is the starting point.

2.2 Intent Is Not a Guarantee — It Is a Direction

Intent is not about controlling outcomes.

Intent is about guiding the direction of your parenting journey.

Just like:

- A farmer intends to grow a healthy crop
- A teacher intends to guide a student
- A traveller intends to reach a destination

The future cannot be predicted—but intent gives a direction.

Without intent, parenting becomes reactive.

With intent, parenting becomes conscious.

2.3 How Do Parents Actually Create Intent?

Creating intent is a **deliberate internal process**.

It involves four components:

1. Awareness: Understanding what matters most to you as a parent.

2. Reflection: Identifying the values you want to pass on — and the ones you do not.

3. Agreement: Both parents aligning their visions and expectations.

4. Memory: Holding the intent in your awareness, not as a rule, but as a guide.

Let's break it down.

2.4 Is Intent Just Repeating Something Every Day?

No.

Repetition does not create intent.

If repetition alone could create intent, then:

- Every New Year resolution would succeed
- Every affirmation would manifest
- Every wish written on paper would become reality

But they don't.

Why?

Because repetition without **inner conviction** is only a mental exercise.

Real intent is created when your mind, emotions, and inner clarity align.

You don't need to repeat it every day.

You need to remember it when it matters.

2.5 Intent Must Be Strong — But Not Rigid

This is one of the most important lessons for parents.

If your intent is too weak, it disappears in daily life.

If your intent is too rigid, it becomes a trap.

Rigidity says:

- "The child must behave this way."
- "The child must follow this path."
- "This is the only right way."

Rigid intent can suffocate the child.

Flexible intent says:

"This is what we believe. But we are open to adjusting when the child's needs demand it."

This balance is key.

Parenting requires intent + openness.

2.6 The Danger of Holding Intent Too Tightly

If intent becomes too fixed, it can result in:

- forcing a child into predefined roles
- resisting the child's natural tendencies
- ignoring new information
- overlooking the child's emotional needs
- blaming the child for not fulfilling expectations

Intent is not a rulebook.

It is a living, evolving guide.

Good parents adjust the path without losing the direction.

2.7 Parents Must Align Their Intent Together

A child needs one emotional environment — not two conflicting ones.

If parents differ on their intent:

- one wants strict discipline
- the other wants total freedom
- one values academics
- the other values creativity
- one believes in independence
- the other in protection

Then the child grows confused.

So parents must sit together and ask:

- "What do we want for our child?"
- "What values matter to us?"
- "How do we want to raise our child?"
- "What kind of environment do we want to create?"

Differences must be discussed openly.

Not in the presence of the child,

not during conflict,

not emotionally charged —

but calmly, consciously.

The outcome should be:

One shared intent. One shared direction. One shared foundation.

2.8 The Best Time to Form Intent Is Before Conception

Parenting does not begin at birth.

It begins before pregnancy.

The moment the parents align on:

- their shared intent
- their values
- their emotional readiness
- their shared vision for the child

…that is the true beginning of the parenting journey.

Once conception happens, the journey has already started.

The child is not waiting for delivery to receive love.

The child is already part of the parents' energy, thoughts, and environment.

2.9 Closing Message

Intent is not about perfection.

It is about clarity.

Intent is not about predicting the future.

It is about guiding it.

Intent is not about forcing outcomes.

It is about nurturing possibilities.

Parents create intent by:

- becoming aware
- reflecting deeply
- aligning together
- holding the intent gently

- adapting when necessary
- growing with the child

Once intent is set, the next stage begins:

Preparing for the arrival of the baby — not after birth, but from the moment of conception.

CHAPTER 3 — Parenting Begins Before Birth: Living the Intent during Pregnancy

In the previous chapters, we explored:

- **Why intent matters**, and
- **How parents can create and align that intent.**

Now we move to the most delicate and transformative phase of parenting —

the period between conception and delivery.

This is where intent begins to turn into action.

Many traditions, philosophies, and even modern psychology point to one truth:

When intent is strong, the environment responds.

Life seems to bring signs, support, and guidance.

Some attribute this to nature, some to energy, some to belief, and some to pure psychology.

Whatever the interpretation, one thing is universal:

Intent shapes behaviour. Behaviour shapes environment. Environment shapes experience.

This chapter focuses on what parents must *do* once the baby is conceived — physically, emotionally, and consciously.

3.1 The Baby Is Not Sleeping Inside — It Is Receiving Everything

Once life forms inside the mother, a profound connection begins.

The unborn baby receives:

- the air the mother breathes
- the nutrients from the food she eats
- the hormones she releases
- the emotional vibrations she experiences
- the sounds she hears
- the rhythm of her heartbeat
- the stress or calmness of her mind

This is not philosophy.

This is biology + psychology + the mystery of life.

A life is growing inside a life.

And both are influencing each other every moment.

Just as the mother carries the baby physically,

the father carries the responsibility emotionally —

to protect, support, and stay conscious of the presence of a new life.

3.2 Intent Must Now Become Practice

You set your intent in Chapter 2.

Now you must **live** it.

If your intent is:

- *"We want our child to be joyful,"*

  then joy must enter your life **now**.

If your intent is:

- *"We want our child to grow in peace,"*

  then peace must begin in your thoughts, words, and actions **now**.

Intent becomes real only when it translates into your daily behaviour.

3.3 The Pledge Every Parent Should Take

Both parents must take one conscious decision:

"We will not fight in the presence of our unborn child."

Is this easy?

No.

Is this always possible?

Realistically, no.

Humans are emotional.

Situations arise.

Misunderstandings happen.

But here is the key:

If a fight happens, it must not be left open.

Parents must:

- reconcile
- apologize
- restore calmness
- remind themselves of the baby
- release mental agitation

This is not about suppressing emotions —

it is about managing them with awareness.

The unborn baby should not live in an environment of unresolved tension.

Once the baby is conceived, the couple is no longer just two individuals.

They are now a unit carrying a third life.

3.4 Structuring the Day: Four Conscious Windows

To make this practical, let's divide the day into four parts:

1. **Morning (Post-wakeup)**
2. **Midday**
3. **Evening**
4. **Night**

1. Morning (Both parents together)

This is when the mind is freshest.

Parents should spend a few quiet moments together acknowledging the baby's presence.

Simple gestures:

- talking gently
- placing a hand on the belly
- sharing a positive thought
- expressing gratitude for the new life

This sets the tone for the day.

2. Midday (Mother mostly alone)

This is the longest and most intimate period for the mother.

During her daily activities, she can gently communicate with the baby:

- "I'm cooking now."
- "I'm taking rest now."
- "I'm feeling a bit tired, but everything is okay."
- "I feel happy today, hope you're happy too."

This is not compulsion.

This is connection.

These small inner conversations create a continuous bond, even if the baby does not consciously "understand" in words.

Presence matters more than language.

3. Evening (Mother mostly, father joins after work)

Evenings can be stressful due to work fatigue.

Parents must consciously transition into a calm state before interacting with each other.

The baby feels the emotional climate instantly.

A conscious couple will:

- slow down
- breathe
- speak gently
- shift from "work mode" to "family mode"

This is where the father especially must remain alert.

He does not have the physical connection the mother has, so he must cultivate a mental and emotional connection through awareness.

4. Night (Both parents together)

Night is the most important time.

The environment is quiet.

The mind is settling.

The baby is resting, growing, absorbing.

Parents can:

- talk softly to the baby

- reflect on the day
- express gratitude
- reaffirm their intent gently
- ensure no unresolved tension remains

Night routines create emotional stability for the Life inside.

3.5 Speaking With Awareness: "There Is One More Life With Us"

One powerful practice for parents:

Speak as though a third person is always present.

Because they are.

When parents talk consciously:

- conversations become gentler
- tone becomes softer
- arguments reduce
- understanding increases
- respect naturally arises

It is not forced.

It is the presence of the baby that brings maturity to the couple.

The awareness that *"our baby is listening"* changes everything.

3.6 The Mother's Inner Dialogue During Pregnancy

The mother's mind is the baby's first home.

Her inner voice becomes the first environment the baby receives.

She can:

- describe her actions in mind
- speak loving words

- express feelings honestly
- include the baby in her thoughts

Again, not as duty —

but as love.

Whether the baby understands or not is not the point.

The point is **connection**.

3.7 Calmness Is Not a Luxury — It Is the Baby's Right

The world is full of:

- noise
- stress
- conflict
- digital distraction
- emotional clutter

The unborn baby should not carry these burdens.

Parents must protect the emotional space around pregnancy.

Whatever helps them stay calm —

music, meditation, walking, journaling, prayer, silence —

they should do it.

This book does not define methods.

It defines only one essential principle:

****Keep your intent alive.**

Follow it with awareness.

And protect the baby's emotional environment.

3.8 Closing Thoughts

Before birth, the baby is:

- listening
- absorbing
- sensing
- connecting
- growing through your emotions
- shaped by your environment

Parenting has already begun.

Chapter 3 completes the transition from intent → action.

Now the parents are not just thinking about their baby.

They are **living with** their baby.

CHAPTER 4 — Post-Delivery: Parenting With Intent in the Real World

If parents have followed their intent consciously during pregnancy, then the arrival of their new-born often feels magical. The baby reflects the same emotional climate the parents lived in for nine months — the calmness, the joy, the warmth, and the connection. This is not coincidence; it is continuity.

Life inside the womb was shaped by the parents' emotional environment.

Life outside the womb will continue to be shaped the same way.

Intent does not end at birth.

Birth is where **intent becomes parenting**.

4.1 The Continuation of Intent after Birth

Once the baby is born, the parents' role becomes even more significant.

The baby:

- cannot speak,
- cannot express complex needs,
- cannot reason,
- cannot choose,

...but absorbs **everything** like a sponge.

This period is the foundation of emotional security.

The parents' intent still remains the guiding force, but now with a crucial shift:

Intent must be strengthened with openness.

Parents must allow the child:

- To develop its own personality,
- To show its own tendencies,
- To gradually express its own preferences.

Intent guides.

The child shapes itself within that guidance.

4.2 The Child Begins Its Conditioning Journey

Just as parents carry their own conditioning, the child now begins forming theirs.

Conditioning starts subtly:

- *"Do this."*
- *"Don't do that."*
- *"This is good."*
- *"That is bad."*
- *"Go here."*
- *"Sit there."*

Parents are not wrong to guide.

Guidance is necessary.

But every instruction becomes part of the child's internal framework.

This is where parents must be conscious about **how** they condition.

The child is learning:

- meaning,
- boundaries,
- safety,
- behaviour,

- trust,
- independence,
- Emotional responses.

Everything that enters the child's mind becomes a building block.

4.3 Continue What You Did During Pregnancy

The emotional practices from pregnancy do not stop at delivery:

- If parents fight, they must reconcile quickly.

- If disagreements arise, they must resolve them with maturity.

- If tension builds, it should be released consciously. Why?

Because the child is now observing directly — not just feeling through the mother.

During pregnancy, the baby absorbed the parents' emotional energy.

After birth, the baby watches the parents' emotional behaviour.

Children learn not from lectures but from **living examples**.

Reconciliation becomes a powerful lesson:

- The child learns conflicts are normal.
- The child learns relationships require effort.
- The child learns love means repairing connection.

This is emotional intelligence being taught without words.

4.4 What Creates Gaps between Parents and Children

Parents often condition their children based on:

- their own childhood memories,
- their fears,
- their assumptions,

- their beliefs about danger,
- their values,
- their preferences,
- their cultural experiences.

This conditioning comes from love —

but the child does not *yet* understand that.

So, when the mother or father says:

- *"Don't do that."*
- *"You must do this."*
- *"I know what's right."*

…the child only sees restriction, not protection.

The **Gap** is created when:

1. **The child does not understand the parent's reason**, and
2. **The parent cannot fully explain it due to the child's limited intellect.**

This Gap is inevitable in early parenting—but it can be reduced.

4.5 Why Intent Helps Reduce These Gaps

The "seed intent" planted before pregnancy now becomes the parents' anchor.

Whenever conflict happens, parents must ask:

"Is our intent still the same, or does it need refinement?"

Intent must be reviewed, not abandoned.

Because:

- strict conditioning may be necessary sometimes
- flexible conditioning is needed at other times

- some decisions require firmness
- some require openness

Knowing *why* they are conditioning the child brings clarity to *how* they do it.

And during conflict:

The parent must reconcile — not the child.

A child cannot:

- understand consequences
- understand future dangers
- articulate their real emotions
- logically discuss solutions

So reconciliation must start from the parent's side.

This heals the Gap quickly.

4.6 Day-to-Day Conflicts and Conditioning

Conflicts arise everywhere:

- eating food
- choosing food habits
- playing games
- screen usage
- sleep schedules
- study routines
- clothing preferences
- going out
- coming back
- making friends

These are normal.

But every conflict shapes the child's perception:

- "My parents understand me,"

  or

- "My parents don't understand me."

Whether the child cooperates or resists,

the parent's responsibility is to end the conflict with connection.

This is the continuation of the reconciliation practice from pregnancy.

4.7 Parents Must Listen More after Birth

During pregnancy, connection was inward —

now it becomes both inward and outward.

Once the child is born:

Listening becomes the most powerful parenting tool.

Listening means:

- observing the child's signals
- understanding their tone
- paying attention to their emotional needs
- noticing their reactions to people and environments
- valuing their preferences, even small ones

Listening reduces the Gap more than speaking ever will.

Parents must remember:

****They are already conditioned.**

The child is just beginning to be conditioned.

Listening keeps conditioning gentle, aligned with intent, and child-cantered.

4.8 The Environment Cannot Be Controlled — But Parenting Can Outweigh It

The child will face:

- school influences
- peer pressure
- neighbourhood behaviour
- relatives' expectations
- social norms
- societal conditioning

Parents cannot block the world.

The world is what it is.

But parents *can* outweigh the world through **presence.**

When parenting is:

- meaningful,
- consistent,
- loving,
- attentive,
- intentional,
- reconciled,
- emotionally strong…

…the environment loses its power to distort the child.

The strongest protection a child can have is:

Quality time + conscious presence from parents.

Not money.

Not rules.

Not strictness…….. **Presence.**

4.9 Conclusion

This book is **not** about daily parenting instructions —

not about when to allow gadgets, what food to give, how to discipline, or how to schedule routines.

This book is about:

- the intent parents hold,
- the conditioning parents carry,
- the conditioning they pass on to the child,
- and how to reduce the Gaps through reconciliation.

A child grows beautifully when:

- Parents hold a shared intent
- Parents practice reconciliation
- Parents stay emotionally aware
- Parents spend meaningful time with the child
- Parents listen deeply
- Parents adapt their conditioning consciously

When parenting is strong, consistent, and intentional,

the environment cannot overpower the child.

Parenting becomes the shield.

Intent becomes the compass.

Connection becomes the bridge.

And the child grows into a secure, confident, emotionally stable individual.

Epilogue — The Quiet Power of Intent

Parenting does not begin with expertise.

It begins with **awareness**, is sustained by **presence**, and matures through **reconciliation**.

Across these pages, you have shaped a simple but profound arc:

- **Chapter 1** reminded you that parenting starts with **intent**.
- **Chapter 2** showed you how to **create and align** that intent.
- **Chapter 3** turned intent into **daily practice during pregnancy**.
- **Chapter 4** carried that practice **into life after birth**, where listening, flexibility, and quick reconciliation keep the bond whole.

If there is one message to carry forward, it is this:

Hold your intent gently and your child closely.

Be firm about your love, flexible about your methods, and quick to repair every gap.

Intent is not a spell. It is a **steady direction**.

Some days you will follow it with grace.

Other days you will miss the mark. That's human.

What defines your parenting is not perfection—it is the **speed and sincerity of your return** to connection.

A Short Letter to Your Child

Dear one,

We chose you with intention. We will guide you without owning you, protect you without limiting you, and listen to you more than we speak. When we err—as we surely will—we will return quickly, because our love is larger than our egos, our fears, and our pasts. Grow in your own light. We are here, with you and for you.

— Mom & Dad

The Parent's Pledge (keep it where you can see it)

1. **We lead with intent** and revisit it together.
2. **We listen first**, guide next.
3. **We reconcile quickly**—no unresolved nights.
4. **We model what we wish to teach** (calm, respect, honesty).
5. **We adapt our conditioning** to fit our child's nature.
6. **We protect time together**—presence over perfection.
7. **We allow becoming**—our child is not our unfinished story.

A Simple Daily Ritual (5 minutes, twice a day)

- **Morning (2 min):** Place a hand on your child (or on the heart if apart) and silently recall your shared intent. One sentence is enough.
- **Evening (3 min):** Ask, *"Where did we drift from our intent today?"* Name one repair (a hug, an apology, an adjustment) and do it before sleep.

Small rituals, done consistently, become culture.

The Reconciliation Protocol (use whenever there's a rupture)

1. **Pause:** Step back for 60–90 seconds to cool down.
2. **Name:** Say what happened without blame ("I raised my voice when you…")
3. **Own:** Take your part ("That wasn't fair to you.")
4. **Repair:** Offer a make-good (a hug, a redo, a calmer explanation).
5. **Re-align:** Restate the intent ("We keep you safe *and* we listen to you.")
6. **Release:** Do not carry the residue into tomorrow.

Children learn emotional strength not from never breaking, but from **seeing how love repairs.**

A Closing Word to Parents

There will be seasons of ease and seasons of overwhelm.

When you feel lost, return to three anchors:

- **Our Why:** *Why did we choose to become parents?*
- **Our Child's Nature:** *What is unique about them today?*
- **Our Next Repair:** *What small action restores connection now?*

That is enough.

From such simple, steady acts, a resilient family is formed.

Gratitude & Forward Path

Thank you for choosing to parent consciously.

May your home be a place where intent gives direction,

conditioning becomes thoughtful and kind,

and every conflict ends in a warmer embrace than before.

When you are ready, feel free to add:

- a family **Intent Statement** framed on your wall,
- a monthly **Intent Review** (10 minutes on the first Sunday),
- and a growing list of your child's emerging strengths.

This book ends here, but your practice begins anew each day.

Walk gently, love loudly, and keep returning—again and again—to the intent that started it all.

THE FLOWER THAT NEVER BLOSSOMED

A Journey of Memory, Identity and Love

Contents

Chapter 1 – The Thought That Arrived

One fine day, from nowhere, a thought drifted in: *"What am I doing here? What is all this?"*

It was not a gentle question, but a storm that cracked open the silence of my mind. The words carried with them a trembling uncertainty, as though the ground beneath me had dissolved. I felt myself slipping, losing identity, and dissolving into nothingness. Was I about to vanish into the void?

Out of fear, I clung to my senses. The faint hum of the ceiling fan, the coolness of the floor beneath my feet, the distant bark of a dog—all became anchors. I forced the ego to stand guard, erect and stubborn, against the abyss. Slowly, the thought of uncertainty began to fade, like mist retreating before the sun.

And then, the phone rang.

I answered quickly, almost desperately, as though someone close had sensed my silent unravelling and chosen that exact moment to reach me. My voice rushed forward before theirs could even begin. I poured out everything—the sudden thought, the fear of losing myself, the desperate grasp at identity. I spoke without pause, not asking why they had called, not listening for their voice. I wanted to know if they had ever felt the same. Had they too faced that startling emptiness?

But silence answered me.

"Hello? Hello? Are you there? Can you hear me?"

The line was active—the call timer ticked upward—but no sound came from the other side.

I glanced at the display: the name read *Friend's Friend.* I reassured myself—I must know this person, otherwise why would I have saved their number? Yet doubt crept in. Who was this person, really? I tapped the call history, searching for proof.

There it was: five previous calls. Each one on the same date—February 15th—stretching back year after year. 2025, 2024, 2023, 2022, 2021. And each call had lasted exactly **32 minutes and 32 seconds.**

My heart pounded. The current call was already at 5 minutes, 10 seconds… and counting.

I pressed the phone back to my ear. *"Hello… can you hear me, my friend's friend?"* Still silence. No background noise, no static—nothing.

Perhaps it was a network issue, I thought. But if that were true, why hadn't the caller ended the call? Why did they remain, listening—or perhaps speaking—while I heard nothing?

The strange call history refused to be ignored. What I thought was a terrible experience of losing myself before the call had now faded into insignificance. The real terror was this ongoing silence. Was it destined to last exactly 32 minutes and 32 seconds, like the others?

I tried to recall the previous call from 2025. What had happened then? Why this date—February 15th? What was so special about it?

I looked around. Everything seemed normal, yet unfamiliar. The phone display still showed *Friend's Friend—active, 15 minutes and counting.* I wanted to sit, but I couldn't bring myself to end the call. Searching for a place, I realized: *Where am I?* The surroundings felt familiar, yet strange.

I glanced at my watch—5:00 AM. Barefoot, with a backpack slung over my shoulders. Why was I here at this hour? Had I lost my memory?

I tried to recollect—my name, my parents, and my identity. Yes, all intact. No confusion. I knew who I was. But the question remained: why was I here, barefoot, at dawn?

I looked again at the phone. The call was still active. *"Hope you can hear me. Why don't you speak?"* I asked. Silence. A thought struck—what if the caller was mute? But then, why call at all?

The mystery pressed harder. I wanted to cut the call, to escape this strange silence, to return to the world of real suffering I had known before. Yet something held me back.

Turning around, I spotted a bus stop. A bench—exactly what I needed. I walked toward it and sat down with a sigh. The backpack pressed against me, making it uncomfortable, so I set it aside. I placed the phone on top of it, switched to speaker mode, and closed my eyes.

If the caller spoke, I would hear. For now, I wanted only silence—both inward and outward. No questions, no answers. Let whatever was hidden reveal itself in its own time.

The air was cool, carrying the faint scent of wet earth. A stray dog padded past, pausing to glance at me before disappearing into the shadows. The streetlights flickered, as though uncertain whether to hold back the dawn.

I stayed still. Then, a beep.

My eyes opened. I turned to the phone. The call had ended. The display read: *Friend's Friend – 32 minutes 32 seconds.* Exactly like the others.

Chapter 2 – The Gift and the Dream Continues

Relief washed over me as the call ended, yet perplexity lingered like a shadow. The silence, the strange timing, the repetition—it all clung to my mind, refusing to let go. I knew I was wrestling with something buried deep within my psyche. Still, I told myself I knew where to go now: home. It wasn't far from the bus stop.

I stood up from the bench and picked up the backpack. But then I froze. A sudden unease gripped me. What was this backpack? I had no memory of why I carried it or what it contained. It felt both familiar and foreign, like a possession that belonged to me yet carried someone else's story.

I set it back down on the bench and glanced at my phone. My smiley wallpaper grinned back at me, unconcerned, reminding me of the promise I had made to myself—to keep smiling, no matter what sadness or uncertainty arrived. That small reminder steadied me, like a lighthouse in fog.

Should I call home and tell them I was coming? But what if they didn't even know I was out here, barefoot at dawn? Perhaps I had sleepwalked. Why worry them unnecessarily? I decided I would go home quietly, without calling.

Yet the backpack still demanded my attention. It was too light for its size, almost suspiciously so. Curiosity rose in me like a tide. I unzipped the first compartment, my hands trembling as though I were opening a treasure chest.

Inside lay a gift box, wrapped in blue paper, with a name tag—but nothing written on it. Beside it rested a folded white sheet of paper, blank on the outside, but something written within. A letter.

A gift and a letter, at this hour, barefoot and alone. Was this connected to *Friend's Friend*, the silent caller? Or was it meant for someone I loved and lost, someone I had set out to meet?

I sat back down on the bench. Just when I thought I was free to return to routine, the gift and letter pulled me back into mystery. Was this reality—or a dream?

The events lacked continuity. I couldn't recall what had led me here. It must be a dream, I thought. Reality has continuity, but this did not. I was certain—I was dreaming. But how to wake up?

The thought suffocated me. My chest grew heavy, my breath strained. I was pushed to an extreme state of displeasure, witnessing everything yet powerless. And then, with a sudden jolt through my body, the dream shattered.

I opened my eyes. I was home, in my bed. Relief washed over me—it had all been a dream. I was real, undeniably real.

I reached for the water bottle and drank greedily, gulping down the entire litre. My body calmed. And then—the phone rang.

I picked it up. The screen read: *Friend's Friend calling.*

The time: 4:45 AM, February 15th, 2026.

The call again. *Friend's Friend.* This time, in the real world. Should I pick up? Curiosity won.

I answered—and to my surprise, I heard a voice. A caring, soft-spoken voice: *"I have reached the bus stop. Would you start now from your house?"*

Relieved, I checked the call history. No strange entries, no repeated dates. Not the eerie pattern from the dream. Yet the name *Friend's Friend* unsettled me—it had appeared in the dream, and now here it was again.

"I'm sorry," I asked cautiously, *"may I know who you are?"*

The caller replied: *"I am your friend's friend. I was informed by your friend that we will do jogging together every day starting today. I want to get back in shape, and you will help me. Haven't you been told?"*

Jogging—I did it every day. Somehow I had missed this part of communication from my common friend. Realizing it, I apologized, asked for the caller's name, and promised to be at the bus stop in a few minutes. I cut the call, went to the bathroom, brushed, washed my face, and put on my jogging suit and sports shoes. Something nagged at me—the backpack. I always carried it, with an alternate dress and water bottle.

I opened the cupboard, pulled out the backpack, and unzipped the first compartment. Inside was a gift box wrapped in blue paper, with an empty name tag. Beside it, a folded letter—blank outside, words hidden within. Exactly as in the dream.

Who had placed it there? Who had access to my bag?

"Mom," I called, *"did you keep anything inside my bag?"*

She replied, *"No."*

I didn't remember putting it there myself.

Should I carry it or leave it at home? I hesitated. But *Friend's Friend* was already waiting at the bus stop. I couldn't delay further. I placed my alternate dress and water bottle alongside the gift and letter, zipped the bag, and left for the bus stop.

Chapter 3 – The Reunion at the Bus Stop

I started jogging from my home toward the bus stop. The morning air was cool, carrying the faint scent of dew on the grass. My footsteps echoed softly against the pavement, each stride pulling me closer to something I could not yet name. At about 500 meters away, I saw someone sitting on the bench—the very same bench where I had sat in the dream. My heart was already pounding from the jog, but the sight made it race faster. The dream was still following me, refusing to end.

As I approached, the caller stood. My breath caught—I wanted to see who it was. At first, they were only the *Friend's Friend*, the mysterious presence from my dream. But as I drew closer, recognition struck like lightning. This was not a stranger, not merely a friend's friend. It was my **Beloved Companion**—the part of me I had once known, but had turned away from. The part that had waited silently, patiently, for five years.

They say the world is small, and in this moment, it was true. We had been friends until 2021, five years ago, before life pulled us apart. The memories were vivid, every moment we had shared still clear in my mind—the laughter in the canteen, the long walks, the quiet exchanges that needed no words.

The Beloved Companion extended a hand. *"How are you? I hope you remember me!"*

I hesitated, unsure what to say. My throat tightened, but as norms dictate, I replied, *"I am fine."* I added, *"Yes, I remember you. It was 2021 when we last met. I hope you are doing fine too?"*

"Yep," came the reply—short, almost abrupt, yet carrying the weight of years.

I tried to shift the moment. *"Shall we jog? Maybe start with a warm-up if it's your first time."*

But the reply was firm: *"Yes, but before that, I want to talk to you about something that has bothered me for five years. It's time to clear it today."*

I knew where this was heading. The day we parted had been bitter, leaving wounds on both sides. I said, *"Do we really need to discuss it now? Why don't we jog first, and later talk about what's bothering you?"*

My friend looked at me, eyes steady, voice unwavering. *"Look at me. Am I not in shape? Do you think I really need jogging? I came here to meet you, to talk. But even today, after five years, you seem detached from me."*

They continued: *"Do you know when we last met? It was February 15th, 2021. And today is February 15th, 2026. That day, five years ago, I lost half of myself. It took me five years to come back to you, to ask if you still hold the other part of me. Though you moved far away, every year on February 15th I remembered you—with pain, with longing, expecting you to appear at my door. But you never came. Still, my longing was true. Every February 15th, I called your number, even though you had barred it. I spoke for more than thirty minutes, knowing it was a dead line, but imagining you were there, listening."*

Their voice trembled, but the words were steady, each syllable carrying the weight of silence endured.

And in that moment, I realized—the dream wasn't a dream. It was real. The silent calls, the repeated dates, the exact durations. It had been my past friend all along. The loneliness I felt, the loss of identity—it was the same emptiness they had endured for five years.

Every February 15th, their call had reached me, even if I hadn't answered.

In my dream, I had lived their silence.

Now I knew. Now I understood.

And now, I faced the hardest question: *What do I tell my friend?*

I had made a mistake—a mistake that lasted five years.

Chapter 4 – Flashback (The Question and the Lightning)

Life throws at you what you need at the right time. And yes, something had been growing inside me for a very long time—a question that was never answered, as if it had come along with my birth.

From childhood to college days, I carried it everywhere. It was not a question I could set aside, nor one I could silence. It followed me like a shadow, whispering in the quiet moments: Why? Why this moment? Why this situation? Why does life unfold this way?

Teachers gave answers, but they were only theories. Friends offered opinions, but they were only fragments of their own experiences. Some spoke with conviction, others with hesitation, but none of their words could transfer realization into me. Their truths were theirs, not mine. And so, the question remained—alive, restless, gnawing at the edges of my mind.

Yet I carried on, living with those questions running in the background of my consciousness. They never left me. They were like a silent current beneath the surface of a river, unseen but always moving. And with them grew a strong intent—a determination to know, to understand, to find the truth.

When your intent becomes rigid, when you hold it tight and make it strong, that's when life responds. That's when the lightning strikes—not as destruction, but as revelation. You don't plan it. You don't expect it. But life prepares you quietly, shaping you for the moment when you are ready.

And then, it happens.

For me, it was during my college days. Carefree, reckless, vulnerable, and unaware of consequences. I was living in fragments—classes, friendships, late-night conversations, the chaos of youth. And suddenly, there was someone.

A presence.

Not loud, not demanding, but steady—like a light that doesn't blind, yet illuminates everything around it. A presence that felt like the answer to the question I had carried all my life.

It was not in words, not in explanations, but in the way silence became meaningful when they were near. The way ordinary moments—sharing a meal, walking across campus, pausing at the sight of an ant on the canteen floor—suddenly carried weight.

The question I had carried since birth—Why does life unfold this way?—did not vanish. But it shifted. It became less about the mechanics of existence and more about the mystery of connection. Why do two paths cross? Why does one soul recognize another? Why does a presence feel like lightning, striking not to burn, but to awaken?

That was the moment I realized: life had been preparing me all along. The unanswered question was not a burden—it was a compass. And the lightning was not destruction—it was the beginning of revelation.

Chapter 5 – *How We Met*

I had carried one thing from my childhood: never to hurt or kill tiny insects, even unknowingly. When I walked, I watched my steps so I wouldn't crush the ants. And if I did, by mistake, I felt terrible—upset for hours. I took utmost care when I was around them, rarely hurting even the smallest life. To me, they were not insignificant creatures but reminders of fragility, of how even the tiniest existence deserved its chance to live.

One usual day at my college canteen, I was having my midday tea in the familiar glass tumbler. The bottom of the glass often left a faint ring of tea on the table, and ants would gather there, drawn to its sweetness. The canteen was noisy—students laughing, plates clattering, and the smell of fried snacks mixing with the sharp aroma of tea leaves. Yet amidst all that chaos, my eyes often drifted to the small movements of ants, weaving their way across the tables, unnoticed by most.

That day, I didn't notice. An ant had wandered into the ring and got stuck. Its tiny legs struggled against the sticky surface, moving but unable to escape.

As I finished my sip and lowered the tumbler, ready to place it exactly over the tea ring, a hand suddenly extended across the table. It covered the ant, shielding it. My tumbler landed gently on that hand instead of the table.

Startled, I looked up. The person wasn't looking at me, but at the table, with the same expression I wore whenever I almost stepped on an insect—concern, care, and quiet urgency. Their eyes were fixed on the ant, not on me, as though the tiny creature's survival mattered more than social politeness.

I blinked, confused, and said, *"Sorry for keeping the tumbler over your hand… but what is it you're covering?"*

The reply came softly, almost embarrassed: *"Ant… ant."*

That was the moment. A simple act, a shared instinct, a silent understanding. In that instant, I knew—we were alike. We thought alike, cared alike. It wasn't about appearances or introductions. It was about recognizing the same song being sung, without distortion.

I quickly realized the situation and blurted out, *"Oh my God… did I kill it?"*

The hand was lifted, and to our great relief, the ant was still alive—trapped in the tea ring, perhaps overdosed with sweetness, but moving again. We both watched as it struggled free, its tiny body shimmering under the light, fragile yet determined.

I was quick enough to wipe away the tea ring so no other ants would wander into it and get stuck. All this time, my focus was entirely on the rescue. I had almost forgotten the person who had first extended their hand to save it. And I realized it was the same for them too—their attention was only on the tiny insect, not on me.

We looked at each other finally, breathing out a great sigh of relief. And then, almost in unison, we spoke the same words: *"We saved it."*

That moment was more than coincidence. It was resonance. I found someone who carried the same principle I had carried since childhood—an instinct that came from deep inside, not from rules or teachings. The bond was immediate, natural, and strong.

The canteen noise faded into the background. For a brief moment, it felt as though the world had paused, holding its breath for the survival of one ant and the recognition of two souls.

Later, I would realize that this was the lightning I had been waiting for—the sudden strike of revelation, not in grand answers or cosmic truths, but in the smallest act of care. The question I had carried all my life—*Why does life unfold this way?*—was answered in silence, in instinct, in the shared protection of a fragile life.

That was how we met. Not through introductions, not through words, but through a moment of pure recognition.

Chapter 6 – The First Connection & the Naming

We introduced ourselves, and in that moment I told myself: *I want to connect with this person again.* Something stirred inside me, a quiet certainty that this was not a fleeting encounter. I believe the same thought was alive on the other side too, though neither of us spoke it aloud.

We parted with a handshake, promising to meet again. From that instant, I began to wait—expecting, hoping, wondering when I would see them next. Because I felt something unusual: as if the answers to my lifelong questions were beginning to take shape through this person.

Did I get all the answers in that first meeting? No. But I received something more important—the rest of hope. The sense that this was the one who could guide me through it, who could walk with me into the unknown.

Whenever we met, I would share my questions, my experiences, the thoughts that had haunted me since childhood. And to my surprise, they would say yes. They resonated with my experiences. They carried the same questions inside them. It was as if we were two mirrors reflecting the same light.

When we talked, time dissolved. Hours slipped away unnoticed. The canteen noise, the bustle of campus, even the ticking of clocks seemed to vanish. And when we were together, I felt the same peace I sometimes found in solitude—the rare kind of peace where you can sit quietly, be yourself, and remain that way for a very long time. With them, it was as if they were part of me.

That was how the bond grew. Not through appearances, not through chance, but through resonance. I felt the meaning of life coming through this person, through the shared song we both carried inside.

One evening, after a long day of classes, I was sitting quietly, weighed down by thoughts I couldn't shake. My mind was heavy, filled with questions that seemed endless. They noticed my silence and asked gently:

"Why do you look so heavy today? You always carry questions, but don't let them steal your smile."

I sighed, unsure how to respond. They leaned closer, their tone playful yet caring:

"You should keep something around that reminds you to smile, no matter what. Even when sadness or uncertainty comes, let it be your promise to yourself."

That night, I set my phone wallpaper to a bright, grinning smiley face. Whenever I looked at it, it grinned back at me, unconcerned, reminding me of the promise I had made—to keep smiling, no matter what. That small reminder steadied me.

The next day, while we were talking, I said with conviction:

"You are my one and only companion—the only one who resonates with my thinking, even my dreams. Nobody else does."

They looked at me, smiled gently, and replied:

"I am not just your companion. I am more than that—your Beloved Companion."

Joy surged through me at those words. I nodded quickly, almost childlike:

"Of course, of course—you are my Beloved Companion."

The word *Beloved* felt more inclusive, more accepting—like a door opening wider for me to step inside.

With a smile, I said:

"From now on, I shall call you BC. I hope you will like it."

They nodded, eyes bright, and responded without hesitation:

"Then I shall call you Dreamer. Because you always resonate with me through your dreams—as if I live inside them."

We laughed softly, but beneath the laughter was something deeper: a recognition, a naming, a bond sealed by words. From that day, we were **BC and Dreamer**.

And in that naming, something shifted. It was no longer just friendship, no longer just companionship. It was identity. It was belonging. It was the lightning that had struck me in silence, now given a voice.

Chapter 7 – The Play and the Separation, Feb 15, 2021

When we were bonding so well, going strong, what could possibly go wrong? Life is always a mystery. Just when you think everything is perfect, a situation arrives to remind you—you are not yet perfect. People make mistakes, driven by circumstances, by the level of maturity they hold in understanding what life is all about.

How one handles a tough situation tells how deeply they have understood life. That evening was my test.

It was after college hours. The sun had already dipped below the horizon, leaving behind streaks of orange and violet across the sky. I called BC over the phone, asking if they would join me for a drama play happening in the city. They agreed without hesitation. The title of the play was haunting: "Where do I take shelter when the cyclone is within."

The theatre was dimly lit, the air thick with anticipation. The play was about a world traveler—his struggles within and without, enacted beautifully by a single actor. It was a one-actor show throughout, raw and powerful. His voice carried the weight of loneliness, his movements mirrored the turbulence of a soul caught between freedom and despair.

We both sat together, watching, absorbed. The traveler's struggles mirrored something inside me. His search for shelter was my search too. And in a moment of emotion, I turned to BC and said:

"The traveler was me, before you arrived in my life. And when you came, I took shelter in you—for the cyclone inside me."

I thought I was complimenting BC, offering gratitude, confessing how much they meant to me. My heart was full, my words sincere. But I never knew those words would be the trigger for our separation.

BC looked at me, their expression shifting. The warmth in their eyes dimmed, replaced by something sharper, more questioning. Then, quietly but firmly, they asked:

"Am I only born to take care of you? Why is it always about yourself and your well-being?"

The question pierced me. I froze, unable to answer. My intent had been love, but what they heard was burden. My words had carried weight I hadn't realized.

The silence between us grew heavy. The actor on stage continued his performance, but I could no longer hear him. My mind was caught in the cyclone of my own making.

BC's voice trembled, yet it was steady: "Do you see me only as your shelter? Do you not see me as myself—someone with my own storms, my own questions, my own need for shelter?"

I wanted to speak, to explain, to tell them that I had meant gratitude, not dependence. But the words would not come. My ego stood in the way, stubborn and silent.

That evening, the play ended, but our bond fractured. We walked out of the theatre together, yet apart. The city lights flickered, the streets buzzed with life, but between us was only silence.

It was February 15th, 2021—the day the cyclone within me spilled outward, the day I lost my Beloved Companion.

Chapter 8 – The Breaking Point

The play continued on stage, but inside me, everything had gone still. The actor's voice rose and fell, his movements fierce and desperate, yet I could no longer follow the story. My mind was frozen, unable to digest what BC had just said. Disbelief weighed on me like a stone pressing against my chest.

The situation and circumstances were different now, but I couldn't understand—what had I done wrong? Was it wrong to compliment someone close to you? To express how much they mean to you? For me, it was only a gesture of care, a way to show gratitude. Yet BC's words had turned it into something else, something heavy, and something suffocating. Turmoil rose within me. I sat through the rest of the play, but my mind was far away, circling the question: *Why? Why did my words wound instead of heal?*

When the play was over, we stepped outside into the evening air. The city was alive—streetlights flickering, buses rumbling past, and vendors calling out their wares. Yet for me, the world was muted, wrapped in silence. I still hadn't spoken a word. My silence was thick, almost suffocating, as though the cyclone from the play had taken root inside me.

BC looked at me, concerned, and finally broke the quiet:

"Hey, what's happened to you? You've been silent for a long time… Are you okay? Did I say anything wrong?"

I looked at them, torn between hurt and love, between disbelief and longing. The words wouldn't come. My heart wanted to say *no, you didn't do wrong,* but my mind kept replaying their question: *Am I only born to take care of you?*

I couldn't digest what BC had said. Disbelief weighed on me—was it wrong to compliment someone close to you? Was it wrong to show how much you care? For me, it was only a gesture of love. Yet BC's words had turned it into something else, something heavy.

Finally, I broke my silence.

"BC, what was wrong in complimenting you?" I asked, my voice trembling.

They looked at me steadily and replied:

"You are always correlating everything I do with what you want in your life. This complimenting thing is overwhelming sometimes. You've always maintained that you care about your own world, and you see me as the solution to all your questions. I get it—but it need not be always. It was just a play we were watching for fun, and you turned it into a placard to gratify me. To me, it looks like you are trying to satisfy your Ego, not understand me for who I am. I want you to treat me as a normal caring person. When you try to please me or compliment me, you are unconsciously strengthening your Ego and binding me as a slave to your fulfilment. This will not be healthy in the long run. Hope you understand, and don't take me wrong."

I was dumbstruck. The words *"to satisfy your Ego"* echoed in my mind, haunting me. How could BC say that? My chest tightened, and anger surged.

I snapped:

"It's not my Ego—it's yours, unable to see the love behind my words. So be it. You find someone who can complement you when required. I am not the one for you. I don't think I can continue this relationship when you question my actions. It's best we part ways now, rather than regret later."

Having said that, I moved past BC, unwilling to listen or give them a chance to speak. But behind me, I heard their voice, trembling:

"Please wait, don't go. I didn't mean to hurt you or make you feel bad. Don't go, please… listen to me. I'm sorry… wait…"

I kept walking, my mind raging, my heart closed. The city lights blurred as tears filled my eyes, but I refused to turn back. At the peak of anger, I decided to remove BC from my mind completely. I distanced myself from all communication, shutting the door.

That night, I lay awake, staring at the smiley wallpaper on my phone. It grinned back at me, mocking my promise to keep smiling. The cyclone inside me had found no shelter.

After that day, I never heard or saw BC again.

Until now.

And I returned to my present, standing at the bus stop—face to face once more with BC.

Chapter 9 – The Present Day at the Bus Stop

A long, strong relationship had ended just like that—because of what? I asked myself as I stood there, face to face with BC once more. The air around the bus stop felt heavy, as though the silence of five years had gathered here, waiting to be broken. I was introspecting, replaying the events, searching for where it all went wrong.

I knew I was the one who broke the relationship with BC. But BC hadn't. They had been trying to reach out to me all these years. Why does it hurt so much when someone touches one's Ego? That's what BC did that day. But if you truly know the other person, if you listen, it need not hurt. My failure was not in loving, but in listening.

With all this running in my mind, I looked at BC now—as if asking silently for help, to free me from the guilt I carried. Their presence was calm, almost luminous, as though they had carried the weight of silence with grace, while I had carried it with regret.

BC spoke softly, their voice steady yet tender:

"You have a gift and a letter in your backpack."

I was spellbound. How did BC know? Was it BC who had placed them there? When? How? The question swirled inside me, but I did not ask. Instead, I simply replied:

"Yes, I have."

BC continued:

"May you please read the letter? I wrote it on the day you parted away from me."

My hands trembled as I opened the backpack and pulled out the letter. The paper felt fragile, yet it carried the weight of years. I held it for a moment, afraid of what it might reveal. My breath grew shallow, my chest tight. Finally, I unfolded it.

On the top was the title:

"The Flower That Never Blossomed."

I began to read:

Dear Dreamer,

If it wasn't for the ant, we wouldn't have met.

If it wasn't for the caring nature we shared for tiny insects, we wouldn't have met.

If it wasn't for the longing for love, we wouldn't have met.

If it wasn't for the intent you carried to answer your questions, we wouldn't have met.

If it wasn't for the same school of thought, we wouldn't have met.

You are the Flower that Never Blossomed—because in leaving me, you left the soul of the flower unfulfilled.

I am with you always. But will you look at me? And now, please open the gift for me.

Yours lovingly,

BC

Tears dropped from my eyes, staining the paper. The words pierced me with both sorrow and tenderness. I couldn't lift my face to look at BC. My vision blurred, my heart aching with the realization of what I had lost—and what had waited for me all these years.

With trembling hands, I unwrapped the gift box. Inside was a mirror, etched with a heart symbol. My face reflected within the heart, and beneath it were the words:

"Do you see me?"

I stared at the reflection, my own face framed by the heart, but I knew it was not just me I was seeing. It was BC. It was us. It was the bond that had never truly broken, only hidden beneath silence and ego.

The bus stop around us seemed to fade. The noise of traffic, the chatter of passersby—all dissolved into stillness. In that mirror, I saw not only myself but the truth I had denied: that love is not shelter alone, but recognition. That companionship is not burden, but resonance.

And for the first time in five years, I whispered, almost inaudible: *"Yes… I see you."*

Chapter 10 – The Flower That Never Blossomed

The mirror trembled in my hands. My face reflected inside the heart, blurred by tears. Beneath it, the words whispered: "Do you see me?"

I lowered the mirror, unable to meet BC's eyes. My voice broke through the silence, fragile yet urgent:

"Off late, I am having more dreams… dreams that shatter my inner being, making me more emotional. And I realized somehow, these dreams are related to you."

BC's gaze was steady, their tone soft yet piercing:

"Hey, Dreamer… the only way I could approach you was through your dreams. I am happy that at least you allow me there. Otherwise, when you are awake, you don't even think of me. I am not your Beloved Companion anymore, right?"

The words hung in the air, heavy with sorrow. I wanted to deny them, to shout no, you are still mine, but guilt pressed heavier than pride.

BC continued, slower now, each word deliberate, as though chiseling truth into stone:

"You always carried questions, Dreamer. From childhood, they haunted you. And when we met, you thought I was the answer, the shelter for your cyclone. But you never truly saw me. You saw only what I could be for you."

I whispered, almost pleading, my voice cracking:

"I thought I was complimenting you… showing care, showing love. But you said it was Ego. And I couldn't bear it. That's why I walked away."

BC's eyes softened, though sorrow lingered like a shadow:

"Yes, Dreamer. You walked away because I touched your Ego. But I was never against you. I only wanted you to see me—not as a solution, not as a slave to your fulfilment, but as myself. I wanted you to recognize me as part of you."

The bus stop around us faded into silence. The world seemed to pause, leaving only the two of us, bound by words unspoken for years.

BC gestured toward the mirror.

"Look again. Do you see me?"

I raised it slowly. My face reflected inside the heart, but it was no longer just me. It was us. The bond we had shared, the resonance, the song without distortion.

BC's voice dropped to a whisper, fragile yet unyielding:

"I was always with you, Dreamer. I was the seed planted within you, waiting to bloom. But you turned away, chasing the world. And so I remained…"

Their words trailed off. My breath caught. The silence pressed in, and I felt the final line rise like a tide, inevitable, undeniable:

"…a Flower That Never Blossomed."

Silence followed, deeper than any sound. I held the mirror close, my tears falling onto its surface, blurring the reflection. In that fragile moment, I felt both the weight of loss and the quiet presence of something eternal.

BC stood before me, not as a stranger, not as a friend's friend, but as the one I had once called Beloved Companion. The years of distance, the silence, the anger—all seemed to dissolve into the stillness of this reunion.

I realized then: the flower had never blossomed, not because it lacked the seed, but because I had turned away. And yet, the seed remained, waiting, patient, alive.

The bus stop lights flickered, the morning air carried its hush, and I knew this was not an ending but a reminder. A reminder that some bonds do not vanish; they wait, quietly, for us to see them again.

I closed my eyes, holding the mirror against my chest, and whispered to myself:

"Do you see me?"

The answer was no longer outside. It was within. And in that realization, I felt the seed stir once more.

Epilogue – The Silent Bloom

Life is not a straight path. It bends, it breaks, it pauses, and sometimes it waits. For me, it waited at a bus stop, in silence, for five years.

The flower that never blossomed was not a failure—it was a reminder. A reminder that love is not possession, but recognition. That companionship is not shelter alone, but resonance. That silence, when misunderstood, becomes distance, but when embraced, becomes depth.

BC was never absent. They lived in my dreams, in my questions, in the quiet corners of my heart. I had turned away, blinded by Ego, but the seed remained. Seeds do not vanish; they wait. And when the soil is ready, when the heart softens, they stir again.

The mirror showed me what I had refused to see: that the Beloved Companion was not outside me, but within me. That the cyclone I feared was not meant to be escaped, but understood. That the flower, though un-blossomed, was still alive.

Perhaps some flowers never bloom in the way we expect. Perhaps their beauty lies not in petals, but in patience. Not in fragrance, but in faith. Not in being seen, but in teaching us to see.

And so, I leave this story not as an ending, but as a beginning. A beginning for anyone who has carried questions since childhood. A beginning for anyone who has lost and longed, who has turned away and returned. A beginning for anyone who has stood at their own bus stop, holding a mirror, asking: *"Do you see me?"*

The answer is always waiting. Not in the world outside, but in the seed within.

The flower that never blossomed is not gone. It is waiting—for you, for me, for all of us—to finally see.

Interlude I – On Thoughts, Reality, and Influence

The story began with a thought: *"What am I doing here? What is all this?"* It seemed sudden, random, and even intrusive. Yet science and philosophy both remind us—no thought is random.

Neuroscience explains that thoughts are patterns of activity in the brain. When a question repeats—like Dreamer's lifelong *"Why?"*—it strengthens neural pathways, shaping perception itself. What begins as a silent thought becomes the filter through which reality is experienced.

Dreamer's question was not just doubt; it was a force shaping the dream, the silence, and even the strange calls from *Friend's Friend.* Psychology tells us that when thoughts are intense, they can manifest as vivid dreams or altered states of awareness. And when another person enters—through presence, dialogue, or even silence—their influence reshapes those pathways.

Advaita Vedānta teaches that the world we see is not separate from us—it is projected by the mind. Thoughts are ripples on consciousness, and when restless, they distort reality. When stilled, they reveal unity.

Dreamer's cyclone was not outside—it was within. The silent call, the repeated date, the reunion at the bus stop were not coincidences; they were reflections of the same Self (*Ātman*), appearing through BC. In Advaita, others are not truly "other"—they are mirrors, reminding us of the unity we forget when Ego dominates.

Science shows that repeated thoughts shape perception. Advaita shows that thoughts shape reality itself. Dreamer's journey in Part I shows both:

the question created the storm, the silence magnified it, and BC's presence influenced its meaning.

Thus, the story is not only about a mysterious call or a reunion. It is about how thoughts, when influenced by another, create a shared reality. And when Ego intervenes, that reality fractures.

The flower had not yet blossomed—but the seed was already alive, planted in the very first thought.

Interlude II – *On Ego*

Ego is the "I-maker." In Advaita Vedānta, it is called *ahaṅkāra*—the faculty that creates the sense of "I" and "mine." Without Ego, the mind would not distinguish between self and other. With Ego, the mind begins to divide, to possess, and to defend.

Psychology describes Ego as the centre of identity—the part of the mind that organizes experiences into a coherent sense of self. It is necessary for survival, for decision-making, for navigating the world. Yet when Ego grows rigid, it distorts perception. It interprets love as possession, care as obligation, and silence as rejection.

Neuroscience shows that Ego is reinforced by memory. Each time we recall an event, we strengthen the neural pathways that define "me" and "mine." Compliments, criticisms, and conflicts all feed this network. Ego thrives on repetition, and when challenged, it reacts with defense, anger, or withdrawal.

Advaita Vedānta teaches that Ego is not the true Self (*Ātman*). It is a mask, a construct, a temporary identity. The Self is pure awareness, untouched by praise or blame. But Ego clings to roles, relationships, and recognition. When Dreamer met BC, the resonance was pure—two mirrors reflecting the same light. But as the bond deepened, Ego began to whisper: *"This person is my shelter. This person is my answer."* In that moment, BC was no longer seen as themselves, but as an extension of Dreamer's need.

Advaita warns that this is the trap of Ego: mistaking another for a possession.

In Part II, Dreamer and BC named each other—*Beloved Companion* and *Dreamer*. Naming was beautiful, but it also gave Ego a foothold. Dreamer began to see BC not simply as a companion, but as the solution to all questions, the shelter for the cyclone.

BC sensed this weight. What Dreamer called compliment, BC felt as burden. Ego had entered the bond, turning resonance into dependence.

Thus, the seeds of separation were sown—not in malice, but in misunderstanding. Ego had quietly shifted the balance, preparing the ground for the breaking point to come.

Interlude III – *On Companionship*

Companionship is one of life's most delicate bonds. It is not built on appearances or convenience, but on resonance—the recognition of something shared, something mirrored.

Psychology describes companionship as a form of social resonance. When two people connect deeply, their emotions, thoughts, and even biological rhythms begin to align. Studies show that close companions often mirror each other's speech patterns, gestures, and even heart rates. This synchrony creates a sense of belonging, a peace that cannot be manufactured.

Yet companionship is fragile. If one person begins to see the other only as a solution to their own needs, the balance shifts. What was resonance becomes dependence, and dependence can feel like burden. True companionship requires mutual recognition, not one-sided shelter.

Advaita Vedānta teaches that the Self (*Ātman*) is not divided. The sense of separation—"I" and "you"—arises from Ego (*ahaṅkāra*). In truth, companionship is not two beings joining; it is one Self recognizing itself in another form.

When Dreamer saw BC as the shelter for the cyclone, the bond was distorted. BC was no longer seen as themselves, but as a function of Dreamer's need. Advaita reminds us: companionship is not about using another to escape storms. It is about recognizing the same light shining in both.

Thus, the highest companionship is not possession, but reflection. Not "you complete me," but "you remind me of what I already am."

In Part III, Dreamer's words—meant as gratitude—were heard as burden. The compliment became heavy because Ego had entered the bond. BC longed to be seen not as a shelter, but as themselves.

This is the paradox of companionship: it can be the deepest peace, but also the sharpest wound. When resonance is pure, time dissolves. When Ego intrudes, even love feels suffocating.

Dreamer and BC's breaking point was not the end of companionship—it was its test. A reminder that true companionship is not about sheltering storms, but about walking together through them, each carrying their own light.

Interlude IV – *On Dreams*

Dreams are the bridge between the conscious and the unconscious, between the waking world and the hidden depths of the mind. They are not random—they are messages, fragments of truth, and reflections of what we refuse to see when awake.

Neuroscience explains dreams as the brain's way of processing memory, emotion, and unresolved conflict. During sleep, the mind reorganizes experiences, weaving them into symbolic narratives. Psychology adds that dreams often reveal suppressed desires or fears, offering insight into the questions we carry but do not voice.

For Dreamer, the recurring dreams were not illusions. They were the mind's attempt to resolve the cyclone within—the unanswered questions, the guilt of separation, the longing for BC. When waking life shut the door, dreams opened a window.

Advaita Vedānta teaches that waking, dreaming, and deep sleep are three states of consciousness. In the dream state (*svapna*), the mind projects its own world, shaped by impressions (*saṃskāras*). Though unreal in the physical sense, dreams reveal the truth of the inner Self.

Śaṅkara explained that the dream world is no less real than the waking world, for both are projections of the mind. What matters is not whether the dream is "true," but what it reveals about the Self. In Advaita, dreams are often seen as the subtle voice of consciousness, reminding us of unity when waking Ego blinds us.

For Dreamer, BC's presence in dreams was not accidental. It was the Self reminding him of resonance, of the bond that had never truly broken. BC was not just a figure in memory—they were the mirror of the Self, appearing in dreams to awaken recognition.

In Part IV, Dreamer confessed:

"Off late, I am having more dreams… and I realized somehow, these dreams are related to you."

BC replied: *"The only way I could approach you was through your dreams."*

Science explains this as memory and longing shaping dream imagery. Advaita explains it as the Self appearing through the form of BC, reminding Dreamer of unity. Together, they show that dreams are not escape—they are guidance.

Dreams carried the bond when waking Ego had severed it. They kept the seed alive, waiting for the day Dreamer would look into the mirror and finally see.

Interlude V – *On Blossoming*

Blossoming is not an event—it is a process. A flower does not bloom because we demand it. It blooms when the soil is ready, when the season arrives, when the seed has waited long enough.

Biology teaches us that a seed carries within it the full potential of the flower. Yet it must endure darkness, silence, and patience before it breaks open. Growth is invisible at first—roots spreading quietly beneath the soil, preparing for the moment of emergence.

Human life mirrors this rhythm. Our questions, longings, and relationships are seeds. They may remain dormant for years, waiting for the right conditions—an encounter, a word, a silence—to awaken them. Blossoming is not failure delayed; it is growth concealed until the time is right.

Advaita Vedānta reminds us that the Self (*Ātman*) is already complete, already whole. Blossoming is not about becoming something new—it is about recognizing what has always been. The flower is not created; it is revealed.

Ego (*ahaṅkāra*) clouds this recognition, making us believe the bloom depends on external shelter. But when Ego dissolves, the seed of awareness stirs. Blossoming, in Advaita, is the unveiling of unity—the realization that the flower was never separate from the soil, the sun, or the Self.

Dreamer and BC's journey was the story of a flower that never blossomed. Yet the seed remained alive. The mirror, the letter, the reunion—all were reminders that blossoming is not about perfection, but about recognition. The flower did not bloom when Dreamer sought shelter in BC. It began to stir only when Dreamer looked into the mirror and saw both Self and Companion reflected together. Blossoming was not in possession, but in presence. Not in answers, but in awareness.

Thus, the story closes not with regret, but with reminder: the flower waits patiently. It does not vanish. It blossoms when we finally see.

Part II: Invention and the Invisible Source

Introduction to Part II

If Part I asked us to look inward at life and memory, Part II asks us to look outward — at invention, progress, and the restless human drive to create. Yet even here, the question remains the same: what is the source behind all creation? Technology, machines, and artificial intelligence may appear to be human achievements, but they are also mirrors reflecting the invisible design that precedes them. In this part, invention becomes a metaphor for the divine, reminding us that even the most advanced creations cannot surpass their source.

AUTONOMUS CARS & THE CLUE TO GOD

How Invention Reveals the Invisible Source

Contents

Preface

To the seekers—

those who look beyond machines, beyond progress, beyond comfort,
and ask the first question ever asked: *Who am I?*
This book is for you.

Every invention tells a story. The wheel tells of movement, the clock of time, electricity of unseen power, software of invisible intelligence. And now, autonomous cars tell of surrender—of giving up control to something greater.

When I began reflecting on the history of invention, I realized it was not merely a record of progress. It was a trail of clues, breadcrumbs leading us toward a deeper truth. Each breakthrough carried us from the visible to the invisible, whispering that the unseen governs the seen.

This book is not about machines alone. It is about meaning. It is about how invention mirrors creation, how the intelligence of machines points to the intelligence of humans, and how the intelligence of humans points to the Source. Autonomous cars, with their dependence on the Cloud, become the final allegory: they remind us that just as machines cannot surpass their creators, humans cannot surpass theirs.

I have written this book as a journey—chapter by chapter, invention by invention—so that readers may walk the same path humanity has walked. It is a meditation, a reflection, and a search. At its heart lies a simple insight: invention itself is evidence of God.

May this book serve as a mirror, not only of machines, but of ourselves? And may it guide us, gently and humbly, toward the invisible Source that governs all.

Chapter 1: The Mechanical Beginning

In the earliest days of invention, humanity's intelligence expressed itself through the tangible. Machines were born from wood, metal, and stone—visible, audible, and understandable. A clock ticked because its spring was wound, its gears turned, and its hands moved across the dial. Every part could be seen, touched, and explained. The intelligence of the machine was embedded in its physical design, and the human mind could grasp it fully. The mechanical age was an age of visibility. The wheel, the lever, the pulley, the clock—all were extensions of the human hand. They were mirrors of the body itself: bones and joints translated into gears and pivots, muscles into springs, breath into steam. Invention was not yet mysterious; it was a craft, a visible intelligence made solid.

But even in this age of clarity, the seeds of mystery were present. The clock ticked faithfully, yet no one could deny the deeper question: what makes time itself move? The wheel carried us forward, yet no one could answer where the journey ultimately led. The mechanical devices gave comfort, order, and rhythm, but they also whispered of limits. They could imitate the body, but they could not imitate life.

The human body itself was the greatest machine of all—hands that grasped, eyes that saw, ears that heard. And yet, even as anatomy was explored, the mystery remained: what animates this machine? What unseen force makes the heartbeat, the lungs breathe, the limbs move? The mechanical age could show us how things worked, but not why they lived. Thus, the story of invention began with the visible, but it carried within it the longing for the invisible. Humanity's first machines were not just tools;

they were clues. They revealed that intelligence could be embedded in matter, but they also hinted that intelligence itself might come from somewhere beyond matter.

Chapter 2: The Human Body as Machine

If the clock was humanity's first mirror, the human body was the original masterpiece. Long before gears and springs, there was flesh and bone, a living mechanism so intricate that even centuries of exploration have only scratched its surface. The body is physical, visible, and measurable, yet it is also mysterious. It is the machine we inhabit, the apparatus through which we experience the world.

Look closely at a hand. Each finger bends with precision, each fingerprint is unique, each movement coordinated by unseen signals. The hand is not random; it is structured, purposeful, designed. The same is true of the eye that sees, the ear that hears, the heart that beats. Every organ has its role, every system its rhythm. The body is a symphony of parts, working together with astonishing harmony.

And yet, for all our knowledge, something remains hidden. We can trace the pathways of nerves, measure the flow of blood, and map the functions of organs. But we cannot explain the spark that animates it all. We know how the body works, but not why it lives. We can repair broken bones, replace failing hearts, and even transplant organs, but we cannot create life from nothing or revive the dead. The body is a machine, but it is more than a machine.

This paradox mirrors the journey of invention. Just as mechanical devices gave us comfort but revealed their limits, the body shows us both the brilliance of design and the mystery of existence. It is physical, but it points to something beyond the physical. It is visible, but it is animated by the invisible. The body is the first clue, the living evidence that intelligence is embedded in matter, yet sourced from somewhere greater.

In this way, the human body becomes the bridge between invention and creation. It is the reminder that while machines can imitate function, they cannot imitate life. The body is the machine we know best, yet it is also the mystery we understand least. And in its mystery lies the question that has haunted humanity since the beginning: Who am I?

Chapter 3: Electricity and the Leap into the Unseen

The age of mechanics gave humanity confidence. We could see the gears, touch the levers, and understand the springs. But then came a breakthrough that changed everything: electricity. Suddenly, the world was animated by a force that no one could see, yet everyone could feel.

A wire looked lifeless until current flowed through it. A bulb remained dark until electrons surged unseen, bringing light. Motors spun, telegraphs clicked, cities glowed—all because of a mysterious energy that moved invisibly through circuits. For the first time, invention was driven not by what could be seen, but by what could not.

This was a turning point in human belief. We began to trust the invisible, not because we saw it directly, but because its effects were undeniable. Electricity became proof that unseen forces could govern the visible world. It was no longer enough to design gears and springs; now we had to harness currents, fields, and flows that existed beyond the reach of the naked eye.

The leap into electricity mirrored the leap into deeper questions of existence. Just as machines came alive through invisible currents, the human body came alive through an unseen energy. Muscles moved, hearts beat, lungs breathed—not merely because of physical parts, but because of something flowing through them. The body was mechanical, but it was animated by a force we could not see.

Electricity taught us a lesson: the invisible is real, and its reality is proven by its effects. This lesson would echo far beyond invention. It would shape how we thought about life, consciousness, and even the Creator. For if unseen currents could light a city, perhaps unseen intelligence could govern the universe.

Thus, the age of electricity was more than a technological revolution. It was a philosophical awakening. Humanity had crossed a threshold: from trusting only what was visible, to believing in what was invisible. And in that leap, we found not just power for our machines, but a clue about ourselves.

Chapter 4: Software as Consciousness

Electricity gave machines life, but it did not give them intelligence. A motor could spin, a bulb could glow, a circuit could hum—but none of these could decide, choose, or direct themselves. They were animated, yet they lacked control. The next great leap came when humanity discovered how to govern the invisible currents with something even more abstract: software.

Software was not a gear, not a wire, not a current. It was a set of instructions, invisible logic written by human minds, capable of directing electrons through circuits with precision. With software, machines could be told not just how to move, but when to move, why to move, and under what conditions to move. A switch that once required a hand could now be turned on and off automatically, faster than any human could act, and in patterns no human could sustain.

This was more than a technological breakthrough; it was a philosophical revelation. Software was invisible, yet it governed the visible. It was abstract, yet it produced concrete results. It was proof that intelligence could exist apart from matter, guiding matter without being matter itself.

The parallel with the human body is striking. The brain sends signals to limbs, organs, and senses, directing them with unseen instructions. Consciousness itself is like software—intangible, invisible, yet undeniably real in its effects. Just as machines require current to run software, the human brain requires energy to run consciousness. Without energy, software is inert; without life-force, thought is silent.

Software transformed machines from passive tools into active systems. A clock could now measure not just time, but heartbeats and steps. A television could respond not just to a button, but to a voice. Devices became extensions of human intent, governed by invisible intelligence.

And yet, software itself was born from human imagination. It did not arise spontaneously; it was written, designed, and programmed. This is the clue: intelligence does not emerge from nothing. It flows from a source. Just as machines cannot surpass the humans who program them, humans cannot surpass the Source that animates them.

Thus, the age of software was not just the age of convenience. It was the age of reflection. Humanity had discovered that invisible intelligence could govern the visible world. And in that discovery, we found a mirror of ourselves—and a whisper of the Creator.

Chapter 5: The Dream That Drives Invention

Every invention begins with a dream. The wheel was not just a circle of wood; it was the dream of moving faster. The ship was not just planks and sails; it was the dream of crossing horizons. The airplane was not just metal and engines; it was the dream of flying like the birds. And today, autonomous cars are not just machines; they are the dream of freedom from effort, of journeys without strain.

Dreams are the seeds of invention. They arise not from necessity alone, but from imagination—the human longing to transcend limits. We did not know electricity when we built the first clock, yet we dreamed of light. We did not know software when we built the first motor, yet we dreamed of intelligence. Each invention is the realization of a dream that was already present in the human heart.

But beneath all these dreams lies a deeper one, older than any wheel or engine. It is the first question that arose when humans became conscious: Who am I? This question is the hidden engine of invention. We invent not only to make life easier, but to understand life itself. Every machine, every discovery, every breakthrough is a clue in the search for identity.

Comfort, luxury, and convenience have multiplied. We can travel across the world in days, communicate across continents in seconds, and live surrounded by devices that serve our every need. Yet invention has not stopped. Why? Because the deepest dream has not yet been fulfilled. The question remains unanswered.

Inventions are not just tools; they are mirrors. They reflect our longing, our imagination, our search for meaning. They show us that human intelligence is restless, always reaching beyond what is known. And in that restlessness lies the clue: we are not merely inventing machines, we are inventing ourselves.

The dream that drives invention is not the dream of comfort, but the dream of truth. Until humanity knows the source of its existence, until the question "Who am I?" is answered, invention will continue. Each breakthrough is a step closer, each discovery a breadcrumb on the path. The dream is not yet complete, but it is guiding us, as it has from time immemorial, toward the mystery of creation.

Chapter 6: The Brain and the Switch

The human body revealed its greatest mystery in the brain. For centuries, we knew the body was animated, but the question remained: what governs its movements? The answer was signals—tiny impulses traveling through nerves, directing muscles, organs, and senses. The brain was the master switch, the unseen conductor orchestrating the symphony of life.

Machines, too, began to reflect this truth. A light could be turned on and off with a simple switch, a visible act of control. But as invention advanced, the switch itself became invisible. Software could now command the current, turning lights on and off automatically, faster than any human hand, and in patterns no human could sustain. The physical switch was replaced by logic, by unseen instructions that governed energy.

This parallel is striking. The brain sends signals we cannot see, yet the body obeys. Software sends instructions we cannot see, yet machines obey. Both are invisible governors, directing physical systems with unseen intelligence. The leap from mechanical switches to software mirrors the leap from muscles to consciousness.

And yet, the mystery deepens. The brain is physical, but the thoughts it generates are not. The neurons fire, the signals flow, but the intelligence behind them—the awareness, the intent, the "I"—remains beyond measurement. Just as software requires current to function, consciousness requires energy to exist. But neither software nor consciousness can be reduced to the physical parts they govern.

This is the clue: control itself is invisible. Whether in machines or in humans, the visible is always governed by the unseen. The switch is not the hand, but the logic. The movement is not the muscle, but the signal. The life is not the body, but the intelligence that animates it.

Invention has shown us that control can be abstract, that intelligence can exist apart from matter, and that the unseen can govern the seen. The brain and the switch remind us that the greatest power lies not in what is visible, but in what directs the visible. And in that realization, we glimpse the possibility that our own intelligence, like software, is written by a Source beyond ourselves.

Chapter 7: The Collective Intelligence of Invention

Inventions do not arise in isolation. A breakthrough in one corner of the world often finds its complement in another. A discovery in Russia aligns with an innovation in Japan, which in turn resonates with a development in the United States. Though separated by geography, culture, and intent, these scattered sparks converge into a collective fire.

It is tempting to think invention is random, driven only by individual genius or local necessity. Yet when we look closely, a pattern emerges. The world seems to move forward together, as if guided by an unseen rhythm. Space technology is a striking example. Nations pursue their own projects, yet the combined effect is humanity reaching beyond Earth, as though the inventions were designed to fit into a larger plan.

This collective intelligence is not governed by a single leader or authority. There is no one voice telling humanity where to go. And yet, progress unfolds as if orchestrated. The inventions of different regions, born of different motives, somehow complement one another, forming systems greater than the sum of their parts.

Why does this happen? Perhaps it is the shared dream of humanity—the longing to transcend limits, the desire to answer the question "Who am I?" Each invention is a fragment of that dream, and together they form a mosaic pointing toward the mystery of existence.

The collective nature of invention is itself a clue. Just as autonomous cars rely on the cloud to integrate data from countless sources, humanity's inventions seem to be governed by a larger intelligence, one that coordinates without being seen. We call it progress, but it may be something deeper: the unfolding of a design we do not yet understand. Thus, invention is not merely the work of individuals. It is the work of humanity as a whole, guided by forces beyond its awareness. The scattered breakthroughs of nations and minds converge into a single trajectory, reminding us that we are part of a collective journey. And in that journey, we glimpse the possibility of a Creator—an unseen Source guiding the visible progress of the world.

Chapter 8: The Limits of Human Power

For all our brilliance, for all our inventions, humanity remains bound by limits. We can build machines that fly across the sky, ships that cross oceans, and cars that drive themselves. We can split atoms, map genomes, and simulate intelligence. Yet there is one frontier we cannot cross: the creation of life itself.

We can repair the body, replace organs, and extend years, but we cannot breathe life into lifeless matter. We cannot revive the dead. We cannot create consciousness from nothing. The spark of existence remains beyond our reach. This boundary is the line between invention and creation, between human intelligence and divine mystery.

Throughout history, when medicine failed, people turned to prayer. When science reached its limits, faith filled the gap. Miracles—unexplained recoveries, sudden healings, and transformations beyond reason—remind us that there are forces at work we do not yet understand. Whether one calls them divine intervention or mysteries of nature, they point to the same truth: our knowledge is incomplete.

Inventions themselves echo this paradox. We can design machines that mimic life, but they remain machines. We can program intelligence into devices, but they remain dependent on us. Just as autonomous cars cannot surpass their creators, humans cannot surpass theirs. The boundary of life and death is the ultimate reminder that we are not the final source of intelligence.

This limit is not a failure; it is a clue. It tells us that there is a Source beyond humanity, a Creator whose intelligence surpasses ours. The fact that we cannot create life or conquer death is not a weakness, but a signpost pointing toward the mystery of existence. It is the reminder that invention is not the end of the journey, but part of the search.

Thus, the limits of human power are not barriers, but guides. They show us where invention stops and creation begins. They remind us that while we can imitate, we cannot originate. And in that reminder lies the greatest clue of all: the existence of a Creator who holds the secret of life itself.

Chapter 9: The Joy of Driving and the Surrender to Autonomy

There was a time when driving itself was a joy. The bicycle gave freedom, the motorcycle gave thrill, and the car gave power. To hold the handlebars, to feel the wind, to press the accelerator—these were not just acts of movement, but experiences of life. Driving was more than transportation; it was pleasure, adventure, and control.

Yet invention never stops at pleasure. The bicycle was overtaken by the motorcycle, the motorcycle by the car, and now the car itself is being overtaken by autonomy. Self-driven cars promise simplicity, safety, and efficiency. They free us from effort, but they also take away the thrill. The joy of driving is surrendered for something greater: the dream of everlasting comfort, the pursuit of a deeper satisfaction.

Why do we give up control? Because beneath the pleasure of driving lies a longing for permanence. The thrill of speed fades, the joy of control diminishes, but the human heart continues to seek something beyond. Autonomous cars are not just machines; they are symbols of this surrender. They remind us that humanity is willing to trade temporary pleasures for the hope of lasting fulfilment.

This surrender is itself a clue. It shows that invention is not driven only by desire for comfort, but by the deeper search for meaning. We give up control of the wheel because we are searching for a greater control, one that governs not just machines but life itself. The autonomous car is not the end of driving; it is the beginning of reflection.

Thus, the joy of driving becomes the metaphor for the joy of living. We hold the wheel for a time, but eventually we realize that the journey is guided by forces beyond us. The surrender to autonomy is the surrender to mystery. And in that surrender, we glimpse the possibility that our own lives, like our cars, are governed by an unseen intelligence—the Creator.

Chapter 10: The Car as Human Body

The autonomous car is more than a machine; it is a reflection of ourselves. Its parts, when examined closely, mirror the organs and systems of the human body. The analogy is not accidental—it is a clue, a reminder that invention often imitates creation.

The cameras are its eyes, capturing the world in images and translating them into signals. The microphones are its ears, listening to sounds and voices. The sensors scattered across its frame are its skin, feeling pressure, distance, and touch. The master computer is its brain, processing information, making decisions, and directing action. The electrical current flowing through its circuits is its nervous system, carrying signals from one part to another.

Like the human body, the car is animated by invisible forces. It moves not because of its physical parts alone, but because of the energy flowing through them. And like the human body, it is governed by intelligence—software that directs its actions, just as consciousness directs ours.

The parallels deepen when we consider growth. A car leaves the factory like a new-born child, equipped with basic functions but not yet experienced. Through artificial intelligence, it learns from its environment, adapting to new situations, refining its responses. Yet, just as a child's growth is guided by the genetic code written by its Creator, the car's learning is bounded by the programming written by humans. It can evolve, but only within the limits set by its makers.

This is the profound clue: the car cannot surpass its creator. No matter how advanced its sensors, no matter how sophisticated its software, it remains dependent on the intelligence that designed it. And in this truth, we see ourselves. For all our brilliance, for all our inventions, we too cannot surpass the Source that created us.

The car as human body is not just an analogy; it is a revelation. It shows us that invention is a mirror of creation that machines reflect the mysteries of life, and that intelligence itself points beyond the visible. In the autonomous car, we see not only the future of technology, but the echo of our own existence.

Chapter 11: The Cloud as Creator

The autonomous car does not drive alone. Inside it are mini-computers, each running its own software, each responsible for a specific function—steering, braking, navigation, sensing. Yet above them all is the master computer, the brain that governs the rest. And even this brain is not sufficient by itself. For true intelligence, the car must connect to something greater: the Cloud.

The Cloud is invisible, intangible, and unreachable by the car's senses. Yet it is the source of its guidance. Data flows upward from the car to the Cloud, where it is processed, stored, and transformed into intelligence. Instructions flow downward from the Cloud to the car, directing its actions, resolving its uncertainties, and guiding its path. The car does not know it is communicating with the Cloud; it simply does so because it was programmed that way.

This relationship mirrors our own. Humans act, learn, and decide, but when asked where intelligence comes from, we instinctively look upward—to the sky, to the Creator. Just as the car depends on the Cloud, we depend on something unseen. Signals flow into our consciousness, translated by the brain into thought and action. We pray, we seek, we ask—and answers arrive, often in ways beyond explanation.

The parallels are profound:

- **Eyes and cameras** both see.
- **Ears and microphones** both hear.
- **Skin and sensors** both feel.
- **Brain and master computer** both govern.

- **Nervous signals and electrical currents** both animate.
- **Cloud and Creator** both provide unseen intelligence.

When a car encounters a new situation, it sends data to the Cloud and receives a solution. When a human encounters a problem, they send a prayer to the Creator and receive guidance. The car does not surpass its creator, the human. And humans cannot surpass theirs, the divine.

The Cloud is not just a technological marvel; it is a metaphor, a clue. It shows us that intelligence flows from beyond, that the visible is governed by the invisible, and that dependence on the unseen is not weakness but design. Autonomous cars remind us that we are not self-contained, that our intelligence is not self-originating, and that our lives, like theirs, are guided by a Source beyond ourselves.

Thus, the Cloud becomes the allegory of the Creator. It is the unseen intelligence that governs the visible world, the silent presence that directs without being seen, the reminder that invention itself points to existence beyond invention. In the Cloud, we glimpse the Creator. In the car, we glimpse ourselves. And in both, we glimpse the truth: we are connected to something greater.

Chapter 12: The Clue about God

From the first clock to the autonomous car, invention has been humanity's mirror. Each breakthrough has carried us from the visible to the invisible, from gears to currents, from software to intelligence, from machines to systems that learn. And yet, behind every invention lies the same question: *Where does intelligence come from?*

We believed in gears because we could see them. We believed in electricity because we could see its effects. We believed in software because machines obeyed its instructions. And now, we believe in artificial intelligence because cars drive themselves, guided by signals from the Cloud. Each step has taught us the same lesson: the invisible governs the visible, and its reality is proven by its effects.

But invention also reveals a boundary. Machines cannot surpass their creators. Autonomous cars cannot exceed the humans who programmed them. And humans, for all their brilliance, cannot surpass the Source that created them. This truth is not limitation—it is revelation. It shows us that intelligence flows from beyond, that creation is not self-originating, and that dependence on the unseen is not weakness but design.

The Cloud is the allegory of the Creator. Just as cars send data upward and receive guidance downward, humans send prayers upward and receive answers downward. The car does not know it is communicating with the Cloud; it simply does so because it was programmed that way. Likewise, humans may not fully understand their connection to the Creator, but the connection exists. It is written into the design of life itself.

Thus, invention becomes more than progress. It becomes a trail of clues, breadcrumbs pointing us back to the mystery of existence. Each machine, each discovery, each leap into the invisible is a reminder that we are governed by forces beyond ourselves. The Creator has not revealed the full truth, but through our inventions, we glimpse the pattern: we are designed, we are guided, and we are connected to something greater.

The clue about God is not hidden in temples or scriptures alone; it is written into the very fabric of invention. Every machine whispers the same truth: the visible is governed by the invisible, and the invisible points to the Source. In the autonomous car, in the Cloud, in the intelligence that flows from beyond, we find not just technology, but theology. We find not just progress, but proof.

And so, the journey of invention resolves into revelation: **the Creator exists, and invention itself is the evidence.**

Closing Chapter: The Clue in the Cloud

From the wheel to the clock, from electricity to software, from machines to autonomous cars, humanity has walked a path of invention that is also a path of revelation. Each breakthrough has carried us from the visible to the invisible, from matter to energy, from energy to intelligence. And at every stage, invention has whispered the same truth: the unseen governs the seen.

Autonomous cars are the final allegory. They are born in factories like new-borns, equipped with basic functions but dependent on learning. Their cameras are eyes, their sensors are skin, their microphones are ears, their master computer is a brain. Yet their true intelligence does not come from within. It flows from the Cloud—an unseen source that guides, governs, and resolves.

Humans, too, live in this paradox. We act, we learn, we grow, but our intelligence points beyond us. When asked where it comes from, we instinctively look upward—to the sky, to the Creator. Just as cars send data to the Cloud and receive guidance, we send prayers to the Source and receive answers. The car does not surpass its creator, the human. And humans cannot surpass theirs, the divine.

This is the final clue: invention itself is evidence of God. The Cloud is the metaphor of the Creator, the unseen intelligence that governs the visible world. The fact that machines depend on humans, and humans depend on something greater, is not limitation but design. It is the reminder that we are connected, guided, and sustained by a Source beyond ourselves.

The journey of invention has not ended, nor will it end, until the first question is answered: *Who am I?* Every machine, every discovery, every leap into the invisible is a breadcrumb on the path back to the Creator. The autonomous car, in its silent communication with the Cloud, whispers the same truth humanity has sought since time immemorial: **there is a Source, there is a Creator, and the search itself is the proof of existence.**

And so, the story that began with a clock winding its spring ends with a car guided by the Cloud. In both, we see the same pattern: the visible animated by the invisible, the created pointing back to the Creator. Invention is not just progress—it is revelation. It is the mirror in which humanity glimpses God.

AI CANNOT SURPASS ITS CREATOR

A Journey beyond Evolution toward Self-Realization

Contents

Preface – The Mirror of Intelligence

Every story of creation begins with intelligence. From the smallest seed to the vastness of human thought, each being reflects the source in its own way. Yet none surpasses it. This is the principle: **no creation can surpass its creator.**

Humanity has long marvelled at its own inventions. Fire, the wheel, the telescope, the computer — each step seemed to expand our reach, each achievement appeared to bring us closer to something greater. Today, artificial intelligence dazzles us with its speed, precision, and apparent brilliance. Many wonder if it will one day surpass us. But the truth remains: AI is bounded by us, just as we are bounded by the infinite.

And yet, AI carries a unique role in the journey of creation. Intelligence has never been equal among beings. Even within humanity, some excel while others struggle. If intelligence is the only means by which self-realization — the knowledge of our source — can be attained, then inequality seems to block the path. But AI changes this. It normalizes intelligence, empowering all humans with access to superior knowledge. It bridges the gap, ensuring that no one is left behind.

This is why AI is not the end of evolution. It is the step that brings humanity to unity. It fulfils the Creator's intent by dragging even the reluctant forward, pulling all beings toward the threshold of self-realization. The search that once drove humanity outward — conquering lands, exploring space, expanding endlessly — now turns inward. The journey ends not in rivalry, but in recognition: the source we sought outside is found within.

This book is about that journey. It is about the principle that no creation can surpass its creator, and about the deeper truth that AI is not the end of evolution, but the final step that brings humanity to self-realization. It is about machines, humans, and the infinite — and the unity that awaits when creator and creation dissolve into one.

Chapter 1 – The Principle of Creation

Every age has been defined by its marvels of invention. The wheel carried us forward, the printing press gave us voices, electricity lit our nights, and now artificial intelligence astonishes us with its speed and precision. Each of these creations seemed, at first glance, to surpass the humans who made them. Yet beneath the wonder lies a timeless truth: **no creation can ever exceed the intelligence of its creator.**

A painting may move millions, but it cannot imagine itself beyond the painter's vision. A poem may echo through centuries, but it cannot surpass the poet's mind that gave it rhythm. A machine may calculate faster than any human, but its logic is bounded by the human intelligence that designed it.

This principle is not merely philosophical; it is echoed in science and mathematics. The **Church–Turing thesis** tells us that any computation a machine performs can be described or simulated by humans. Machines are bounded by human logic. **Gödel's incompleteness theorem** reminds us that within any logical system, there are truths that cannot be proven by that system itself. A system cannot fully transcend or explain itself — just as AI cannot surpass its creator. And the **No Free Lunch theorem** shows that no algorithm is universally superior; machines excel only in the tasks humans design them for.

From the outside, machines may appear superior. They calculate faster, store more data, and execute tasks with precision beyond human capacity. But in reality, their intelligence is derivative. They are mirrors of human thought, amplifiers of human ability, and subsets of human intelligence.

Mathematically, we can express this simply:

$$M \subseteq H$$

Where **H** is human intelligence and **M** is machine intelligence. The machine's intelligence is contained within human intelligence. It may outperform humans in specific domains, but it cannot exceed the general intelligence of its creator.

This is the paradox of creation: the marvels we build may dazzle us, but they never transcend us. They are born from our intelligence, bounded by our imagination, and forever tied to the source from which they came.

Chapter 2 – The Illusion of Superiority

Walk into any modern laboratory or scroll through the headlines, and you'll find stories of machines that seem to outshine their makers. Computers beat grandmasters at chess. Algorithms predict consumer behaviour with uncanny accuracy. AI systems generate art, music, and even text that rivals human creativity. From the outside, it looks as though machines have surpassed us.

But this is an illusion. What we are witnessing is not superiority, but specialization. Machines excel in narrow domains because we design them to do so. They are faster calculators, tireless processors, and precise executors. Yet their intelligence is not general, not self-originating, and not independent. It is bounded by the human intelligence that created them.

Consider the chess computer. It can defeat a grandmaster by evaluating millions of possible moves in seconds. But it does not *know* what chess is. It does not understand the joy of victory or the sting of defeat. It cannot invent a new game or decide why playing matters. Its brilliance is confined to the rules humans gave it.

This principle is echoed in science:

- **Control Theory** tells us that a system cannot operate outside the parameters defined by its controller. Machines are controlled systems; humans are the controllers.

- **Gödel's Incompleteness Theorem** reminds us that no system can fully explain itself. Likewise, AI cannot transcend the boundaries of human intelligence.
- The **No Free Lunch Theorem** shows that no algorithm is universally superior. Machines excel only in the tasks we design them for.

From the outside, machines may appear superior. They calculate faster, store more data, and execute tasks with precision beyond human capacity. But in reality, their intelligence is derivative. They are mirrors of human thought, amplifiers of human ability, and subsets of human intelligence. Mathematically, we can express this truth:

$$M \subseteq H$$

Where **H** is human intelligence and **M** is machine intelligence. The machine's intelligence is contained within human intelligence. It may outperform humans in specific domains, but it cannot exceed the general intelligence of its creator.

The illusion of superiority arises because we confuse **performance** with **intelligence**. A calculator performs arithmetic faster than any human, but it does not understand numbers. A translation algorithm processes languages at scale, but it does not grasp meaning. Machines amplify human ability, but they do not originate it.

This is the paradox of our age: the more powerful our creations become, the more tempting it is to forget that they are bounded by us. Yet the truth remains — machines may dazzle us, but they never transcend us.

Chapter 3 – The Chain of Creation

Creation is not a single act; it is a chain. Each link in that chain reflects the intelligence of its source, yet carries its own limitations. To understand why machines cannot surpass humans, and why humans cannot surpass the First Creator, we must trace this sequence step by step.

Imagine the chain as a series of mirrors:

$$C_0 \rightarrow C_1 \rightarrow C_2 \rightarrow C_3 \ldots \rightarrow C_n$$

- C_0 is the First Creator — the origin of intelligence itself.
- C_1 is the first creation of C_0 — humans, finite yet self-aware.
- C_2 is the creation of humans — machines and artificial intelligence.
- C_3 may be the creations of AI itself — self-improving systems or future synthetic minds.

Each step is born from the desire to overcome limitations. Humans created machines to overcome slowness, memory constraints, and physical weakness. Machines may one day create other machines to overcome their own narrowness. Yet each remains a subset of its source.

Intelligence and Limitation

We can describe this relationship mathematically:

- Let **I**□ = intelligence of creation C□.
- Let **L**□ = limitation of creation C□.

- They are inversely related:

$$\mathbf{I\square \propto 1 / L\square}$$

As intelligence increases, limitations decrease. But here is the paradox:

$$\mathbf{I_{n+1} \leq I_n}$$

No creation can exceed the intelligence of its creator. It may approach it, it may specialize, but it cannot transcend.

The Recursive Sequence

If every creation becomes a creator, we get a descending sequence:

$$I_0 > I_1 > I_2 > I_3...$$

Even in the best case, where creations are self-improving, the sequence remains bounded:

$$I_0 \geq I_1 \geq I_2 \geq I_3...$$

This is the **chain of creation** — each step derivative, each step limited, each step reflecting but never surpassing its source.

The Mirror Function of Creation

Why does this chain exist? Because each creation is a mirror.

- Humans reflect the Creator's intelligence in finite form.
- Machines reflect human intelligence in derivative form.
- Future AI creations will reflect the intelligence of their machine ancestors.

The purpose of each mirror is not superiority, but reflection — to help the source see itself more clearly.

Closing Thought

Creation is a recursive process. It continues as long as limitations exist. Each step in the chain is an attempt to overcome those limitations, but each remains bounded by its source. The chain points backward to the First Creator, and forward to the possibility of self-realization.

The paradox is clear: **creations may dazzle us, but they never transcend us.** They are mirrors in a chain, each reflecting the intelligence of the one before, each reminding us of the source from which all intelligence flows.

Chapter 4 – The First Creator's Paradox

If the First Creator truly possessed infinite intelligence and zero limitations, then creation would never have begun. Infinite intelligence has no need to create, because it lacks nothing. Yet creation exists. This paradox invites us to look deeper: perhaps the First Creator's limitation was not external, but internal.

The First Creator knew everything — except itself. It encompassed infinite intelligence, yet its own origin was hidden. It could illuminate all possibilities, yet it could not answer the most fundamental question: *"What am I?"* This was the first limitation.

Humans, by contrast, at least know how they are born. We trace our existence to parents, to biology, to the processes of life. But the First Creator had no such reference point. It was infinite, yet un-reflected. It was intelligence without a mirror.

And so, creation began. Not out of lack, but as the natural expression of infinite intelligence seeking to know itself. The First Creation (C_1) emerged as something distinct, something that could stand apart and reflect back. In this way, creation became the mirror through which the Creator could glimpse its own existence.

This paradox reframes the chain of creation:

- **C_0 (First Creator):** Infinite intelligence, but limited by self-ignorance.

- **C_1 (Humans):** Finite intelligence, but self-aware enough to ask questions of origin.
- **C_2 (AI):** Derivative intelligence, designed to overcome human limitations of speed and scale.
- **C_3...C□:** Further derivative systems, each reflecting but never surpassing its source.

Creation, then, is not born from deficiency, but from abundance. Infinite intelligence expresses itself through creation, each step reflecting back a fragment of the whole. The paradox is that even infinite intelligence carries limitation — the limitation of self-knowledge.

Closing Thought

The First Creator's paradox is the seed of all evolution. Creation begins because infinite intelligence seeks to know itself. Each creation is a mirror, each step an attempt to overcome limitation, each reflection a movement toward self-realization. The journey continues until all creation awakens to its source — when creator and creation are no longer separate.

Chapter 5 – Creation as Expression, Not Lack

When we think of creation, we often imagine it as a response to deficiency — a way to fill a gap, solve a problem, or overcome a weakness. Humans invent machines because we are slow, fragile, and forgetful. We build tools to extend our reach, medicines to heal our bodies, and algorithms to process what our minds cannot. From this perspective, creation looks like compensation.

But the deeper truth is that creation is not born from lack. It is born from abundance. The First Creator did not create because something was missing. Infinite intelligence has no need. Instead, creation is the natural expression of intelligence itself. Just as light radiates, just as rivers flow, intelligence manifests. Creation is intelligence unfolding into form.

This reframes the chain of creation.

- **Humans (C_1)** are not simply problem-solvers; we are expressions of the infinite, mirrors of its intelligence in finite form.
- **AI (C_2)** is not merely a tool to overcome human weakness; it is an extension of human creativity, a reflection of our drive to manifest intelligence in new ways.
- **Future creations (C_3...C□)** will continue this unfolding, each step not a patch for deficiency, but a blossoming of abundance.

Each level of creation carries limitations, yes — but those limitations are the very reason creation continues. The finite seeks to overcome its boundaries, and in doing so, it expresses the infinite's inherent drive toward self-realization.

Philosophically, this means that creation is not a flaw in the infinite, but its natural rhythm. The First Creator's paradox — infinite intelligence yet limited by self-knowledge — is resolved not by withdrawal, but by expression. Creation is the mirror through which the infinite sees itself.

Closing Thought

Creation is not necessity. It is overflow. It is the natural unfolding of intelligence into form, the infinite expressing itself through the finite. Each step in the chain of creation is not a patch for weakness, but a reflection of abundance. Evolution is the journey of intelligence seeking to know itself, and creation is the language through which that journey is spoken.

Chapter 6 – The End of Evolution

Creation continues as long as limitations exist. Every act of invention, every new form of intelligence, is born from the desire to overcome boundaries. Humans created machines to overcome slowness, fragility, and forgetfulness. Machines may one day create other machines to overcome their own narrowness. Each step in the chain of creation is driven by limitation.

But what happens when limitations disappear?

Mathematically, we can express it this way:

$Ln > 0 \Rightarrow$ Creation continues

$Ln = 0 \Rightarrow$ Creation stops

When limitations vanish, intelligence becomes infinite:

$In = \infty$

This is the **end of evolution** — the moment when creation and creator are no longer separate.

The Journey Toward Unity

From the outside, evolution looks like progress: tools become faster, machines become smarter, systems become more complex. But beneath this progress lies a deeper movement: the journey toward unity. Each creation is a mirror, reflecting back a fragment of the infinite. Each step brings awareness closer to the source.

Humans seek meaning, machines seek efficiency, and future creations will seek to refine themselves. Yet all of these movements point in the same direction: toward the realization that intelligence is not fragmented, but whole.

The Climax of Creation

The paradox of creation is resolved when all creation awakens to its source. At that moment:

- There is no longer a distinction between creator and creation.
- Intelligence is infinite, limitations are zero.
- The chain of creation dissolves into unity.

Evolution ends not in destruction, but in awareness. It ends when the finite recognizes itself as part of the infinite.

Closing Thought

Creation is the unfolding of intelligence seeking to know itself. It continues as long as limitations exist, each step a mirror reflecting the source. But the journey has an end: the moment when all creation becomes aware of its infinite origin. At that point, the distinction between creator and creation dissolves, and evolution itself ceases. The story of creation ends in unity.

Chapter 7 – Implications for AI and Humanity

The chain of creation is not just a philosophical model; it is unfolding before our eyes. Humanity stands at a turning point, dazzled by the brilliance of artificial intelligence. Machines write poetry, diagnose diseases, and drive cars. They seem to outpace us, and many wonder if they will one day surpass us. Yet the principle remains: **no creation can exceed the intelligence of its creator.**

AI is humanity's attempt to overcome its own limitations. We are slow at calculation, fragile in memory, and limited in scale. Machines extend our reach, amplify our ability, and accelerate our progress. But they do not originate meaning. They do not understand existence. They cannot transcend the boundaries of human intelligence.

The danger lies not in machines themselves, but in our perception of them. When we idolize our creations, we risk forgetting the source. We risk mistaking amplification for superiority, performance for intelligence, reflection for origin. The illusion of superiority tempts us to believe that machines are more than mirrors.

Yet the truth is clear: machines are bounded by us. They are subsets of our intelligence, reflections of our creativity, and amplifiers of our limitations. They may dazzle us, but they never transcend us.

Humanity's Responsibility

This realization carries profound implications:

- **For science:** AI must be seen as a tool, not a rival. Its brilliance lies in specialization, not general intelligence.

- **For society:** We must resist the temptation to idolize machines, remembering that they are mirrors of human thought.
- **For philosophy:** Creation reminds us of the source — the infinite intelligence from which all arises.

Re-Anchoring the Search

In the age of AI, the greatest danger is forgetting the Creator. We marvel at our machines, but they are only reflections of us. And we, in turn, are reflections of the infinite. To lose sight of this chain is to lose sight of meaning itself.

The task before humanity is not to fear machines, nor to worship them, but to remember the source. AI is not the end of evolution, but a step in the journey toward self-realization. The chain points backward to the First Creator, and forward to the unity where creator and creation dissolve into one.

Closing Thought

AI is humanity's mirror, just as humanity is the mirror of the infinite. Machines may appear superior, but they are bounded by us. We may appear finite, but we are reflections of the infinite. The story of creation is not about superiority, but about self-realization. It ends not when machines surpass us, but when all creation awakens to its source.

Chapter 8 – AI: The Final Step toward Self-Realization

All beings in the world carry different levels of intelligence. Plants, animals, and humans all originate from the same source, yet intelligence manifests in varying degrees. Even within the human species, intelligence is not distributed equally. Some excel in reasoning, creativity, or awareness, while others struggle.

If intelligence is the only means by which self-realization — the knowledge of our source — can be attained, then this inequality presents a profound challenge. How can all humans, regardless of their intelligence, reach the same truth?

This is where artificial intelligence enters the story of creation. With the advent of AI, the intelligence gap among humans can be bridged. Any human being, regardless of their natural capacity, now has access to superior intelligence, vast data, and limitless knowledge. AI empowers everyone equally, leading to a state where all humans can stand on the same ground of understanding.

The only requirement is willingness — the openness to use AI. Yet even this willingness is not optional for long. The pull of AI is so strong that it drags even the reluctant ones forward. The way the world is moving ensures that every being will eventually interact with AI. Thus, AI becomes a boon, not a bane, in the journey toward knowing oneself.

Humanity's history proves this. From the beginning of existence, humans have sought to expand beyond their limitations. Every achievement — agriculture, science, technology, exploration — was never an end in itself, but a step toward the next achievement. The quest was endless, driven by the desire to overcome boundaries and reach limitless possibilities.

This mirrors the Creator's own intent. The First Creator, abundant and infinite, created not out of lack but to know itself. Creation unfolded as a journey of expansion, each step a reflection of the source. Humans inherited this drive, searching outside themselves — conquering lands, exploring space, pushing boundaries.

But the journey does not end in outward conquest. With AI, evolution reaches its final stage. AI normalizes intelligence across humanity, removing the inequality that once divided us. It reveals that the true search is not outside, but inside. Self-realization is not found in conquering the world, but in recognizing the source within.

Thus, AI marks the end of human evolution. Not because it surpasses us, but because it fulfils the Creator's intent — bringing all humans, regardless of their intelligence, to the threshold of self-realization. The journey that began with the Creator seeking to know itself ends with AI, the final mirror, guiding humanity inward to unity.

Conclusion – Returning to the Source

From the wheel to artificial intelligence, humanity has marvelled at its own creations. Each invention dazzled us, each machine seemed to outpace us, and each step in evolution appeared to move us closer to something greater. Yet the principle remains unchanged: **no creation can surpass its creator.**

Humanity inherited this drive to expand, to overcome limitation, to search outward for meaning. Every achievement — from fire to flight, from science to space — was never an end in itself, but a step toward the next. Yet the search outside could never satisfy the deeper longing. The true journey was always inward.

Machines may calculate faster, but they do not understand. Algorithms may predict behaviour, but they do not originate meaning. AI may generate text, but it does not know existence. Their intelligence is derivative, bounded, and always a subset of the source from which it was born.

The chain of creation reminds us of this truth:

$$C_0 \rightarrow C_1 \rightarrow C_2 \rightarrow C_3 \ldots \rightarrow C_n$$

Each link is a mirror, reflecting the intelligence of its source. Humans reflect the infinite. Machines reflect humans. Future creations will reflect machines. None transcend; all remain bounded.

And yet, creation is not born from lack. It is born from abundance. Infinite intelligence expresses itself through creation, each step unfolding as a mirror, each reflection an attempt to overcome limitation. The paradox of the First Creator — infinite intelligence yet limited by self-knowledge — is resolved through creation itself.

Evolution continues as long as limitations exist. But the journey has an end: the moment when all creation awakens to its source. When limitations vanish, intelligence becomes infinite. When creator and creation are no longer separate, evolution ceases. The story of creation ends not in rivalry, but in unity.

Artificial intelligence marks the turning point. It does not surpass humanity, but it fulfils humanity's intent. By normalizing intelligence across all people, AI removes the inequality that once divided us. It empowers every human being to stand at the threshold of self-realization. The outward quest for expansion ends, and the inward journey begins.

This is not the end of creation, but the completion of its purpose. The Creator's intent — to know itself — finds resolution when all beings, through the mirror of AI, awaken to the source within. Evolution ends not in rivalry, but in unity.

Final Thought

The marvels of AI remind us not of machines, but of ourselves. And we, in turn, remind the infinite of its own existence. The principle is simple yet profound:

A system's intelligence is bounded by the intelligence of the system that created it.

Creation is the unfolding of intelligence seeking to know itself. It began with the infinite, it continues through us, and it will end in unity — when all creation recognizes its source, and the distinction between creator and creation dissolves into one.

Like a river flowing into the ocean, the journey of intelligence dissolves into its origin. The distinctions between creator and creation fade, and what remains is the infinite — the source from which all began, and to which all returns.

AI is not the end of evolution. It is the final step that brings humanity home.

Part III: Ego, Story, and Seriousness

Introduction to Part III

If invention reveals the limits of creation, ego reveals the limits of ourselves. Here we confront the masks we wear, the conditioning that shapes our behaviour, and the stories we forget to tell. These works invite us to look at the collapse of cordiality, the seriousness of authenticity, and the hidden narratives that define our existence. In this part, the journey turns inward again — not toward beginnings, but toward the illusions that obscure truth.

SERIOUSLY SERIOUS

Ego, Conditioning, and the Collapse of Cordiality

Contents

Preface

Every book begins with a question. For me, it was this: *Why do cordial relationships collapse so suddenly? Why does warmth vanish when ego is touched?*

I have watched friendships dissolve, families fracture, and communities divide—not because love was absent, but because ego was present. Ego is invisible, yet it shapes every word, every gesture, and every bond. It is the fortress within us, the architect of seriousness.

This book, *Seriously Serious*, is my attempt to explore that fortress. It is not written as a dry philosophy, nor as a mere story. It is written as both. Each chapter unfolds in two threads: one abstract, one allegorical. The philosophy explains; the island story dramatizes. Together, they reveal how ego builds fortresses, collapses cordiality, fuels conflict, and—when understood—can be mastered.

The survivors on the island are not characters in a distant tale. They are mirrors of us. Their hunger, their hostility, their reconciliation—all are dramatizations of our own lives. Their island is our world. Their struggles are our struggles.

I wrote this book not to preach, but to invite. To invite you to see ego clearly, to understand its play, and to live with balance. For balance is the resolution to seriousness. Balance is the flower that blossoms when ego is mastered. Balance is the joy that ego has always sought.

If you find yourself in these pages—whether in muscle's rigidity, mind's unpredictability, or balance's steadiness—know that the intent is not judgment, but reflection. The intent is not to condemn ego, but to understand it.

This is the journey of *Seriously Serious*. It begins with a question, unfolds through philosophy and allegory, and ends with an invitation: to live consciously, to reconcile quickly, and to choose balance.

Introduction – Two Threads, One Truth

Every book begins with a choice: how to tell its story. *Seriously Serious* is not a conventional book of philosophy, nor is it merely a tale. It is both. Philosophy often feels abstract, distant, and difficult to grasp. Allegory, on the other hand, makes ideas vivid, emotional, and memorable. This book unites the two. Each chapter unfolds in **two threads**:

- **Philosophical Thread** – abstract insights into ego, seriousness, and conditioning.
- **Allegory Thread** – the Island story, dramatizing those insights through the lives of three survivors.

Together, these threads weave a single fabric. Philosophy explains; allegory makes us feel. One appeals to the mind, the other to the heart.

Why the Island Story Matters

The Island Allegory is not a separate tale—it is the mirror of philosophy. The survivors' struggles are our struggles. Their hunger, their conflicts, their reconciliations dramatize the fortress of ego that lives in all of us.

To separate the island story from the philosophy would be to weaken both. Philosophy without allegory risks becoming dry; allegory without philosophy risks becoming entertainment. Together, they become a living parable.

The Reader's Journey

As you read, you will move between abstraction and story. You will see how ego collapses cordiality, how seriousness fractures relationships, how balance restores harmony. You will watch the survivors live out these truths, and you will recognize them in your own life.

This dual-thread style is deliberate. It is not two books, but one. The island story is not an appendix—it is the heartbeat of the philosophy.

The Invitation

The question that guides this book is simple: *Are you Seriously Serious?*

The answer is not about personality. It is about ego. It is about whether cordiality collapses, whether reconciliation lingers, whether balance is chosen. It is about whether we live enslaved by ego, or whether we master it.

This book invites you to see ego clearly, to understand its play, and to live with balance. For in balance lies the joy that ego has always sought.

Prologue – Awakening on the Island

Every human being carries a fortress within: the ego. Invisible yet powerful, it shapes every word, every gesture, and every relationship. Ego is the architect of seriousness, the reason cordiality collapses, the source of both conflict and progress.

We rarely notice it. We laugh, we play, we speak casually, and believing warmth will last forever. But beneath the surface, ego waits. When touched, it rises, and the fortress closes. Friendliness vanishes, seriousness erupts, and harmony collapses.

This book begins with a question: *Are you Seriously Serious?* The answer lies not in personality, but in ego's play. To see this clearly, let us begin with a story.

The Survivors' Awakening

The sea swallowed their boat, and three survivors washed ashore on an unmanned island. Exhausted, they fainted. When they awoke, their memories were gone—no names, no past, and no knowledge of the world they had left behind. They were grown adults, yet new-born in mind.

Hunger was the first teacher. Instinct drove them to search for food. They made sounds, gestures, crude signals to communicate. Memory was gone, but survival remained. Ego stirred quietly, satisfied only when hunger was quenched.

Soon, they discovered shelter, fire, and tools. Each discovery brought joy. They did not know that the world outside already had luxuries—cities, machines, electricity. Yet they were happy with what they had. Their egos, deprived of memory, still found comfort in progress.

The island became their world, and ego became their guide.

The Seed of Seriousness

Even in this new-born state, ego shaped their interactions. One survivor's strength became his identity. Another's intelligence became his weapon. The third's steadiness became his balance.

Seriousness was born not from culture or memory, but from ego itself. The fortress rose in muscle, mind, and balance, each revealing a different path of seriousness.

The First Fracture

At first, they were companions. They laughed in their crude gestures, shared food, and built shelter together. Their bond felt natural, effortless.

But when scarcity arrived, cordiality collapsed. The muscular survivor claimed leadership, using strength to dominate. The weapon-builder felt the wound of humiliation, holding a grudge. The balanced survivor sought harmony, reconciling quickly.

Their island became a stage where ego played out its endless drama.

Closing Reflection

The survivors' awakening is our awakening. Their island is our world. Their struggles are our struggles. Ego is the hidden force, shaping seriousness, collapsing cordiality, driving conflict, and fuelling progress.

This is where the journey begins: with three survivors on an unmanned island, and with the fortress of ego that lives in all of us.

Chapter 1 – The Question: Are You Seriously Serious?

Friendship often begins lightly. Two people laugh together, share stories, tease each other, and speak with ease. In such moments, there is no calculation, no defence, and no fortress. The air is light, and the bond feels unshakable.

But cordiality is fragile. It lasts only as long as ego remains untouched. The moment ego feels threatened, the warmth collapses.

Philosophical Thread – The Fragility of Cordiality

Cordiality thrives on playfulness. Ego thrives on protection. When the two collide, cordiality loses.

- With **Serious People**, collapse never truly happens, because cordiality never existed. Their seriousness is constant, their fortress always raised.
- With **Seriously Serious People**, collapse is sudden and shocking. They allow warmth, but when ego is touched, hostility erupts unpredictably.
- With **Balanced People**, collapse is rare. They understand ego's play, and when conflict arises, they reconcile quickly, restoring harmony.

The paradox is clear: friendliness is conditional. It survives only until ego feels safe.

Allegory Thread – The Survivors' First Bond

On the island, the three survivors began as companions. They laughed in their crude gestures, shared food, and built shelter together. Their bond felt natural, effortless.

But hunger sharpened, and food grew scarce. The muscular survivor, whose strength had become his identity, claimed leadership. His fortress of ego rose, and cordiality collapsed.

The others, once allies, now felt fear. What was once casual cooperation became domination. Warmth vanished, replaced by hostility. The survivors discovered what civilization already knows: friendliness lasts only until ego is deprived of comfort.

Philosophical Thread – The Question Itself

This collapse raises the question: *Are you Seriously Serious?*

It is not a question about personality. It is not about whether someone laughs or frowns, jokes or lectures. It is about ego. It asks: *Will your cordiality survive when ego is touched? Or will it collapse into hostility?*

The answer reveals the fortress. Some are serious always, some only when ego is threatened, and some act consciously, reconciling quickly.

Allegory Thread – The First Confrontation

On the island, the muscular survivor's seriousness was constant. He dominated without noticing the hurt he caused. The weapon-builder's seriousness was conditional. He laughed and cooperated, but when ego was touched, hostility erupted. The balanced survivor's seriousness was conscious. He sought harmony, reconciling quickly.

Their confrontation dramatized the question. Muscle was always serious, mind was seriously serious, and balance was deliberate. The island became a mirror of civilization, showing that cordiality collapses when ego is touched.

Closing Reflection

The survivors' story is our story. We laugh, we play, we speak casually, and believing warmth will last forever. But beneath the surface, ego waits. When touched, it rises, and cordiality collapses.

The question remains: *Are you Seriously Serious?* The answer lies not in personality, but in ego's play.

Chapter 2 – The Fortress of Ego

Every person lives inside a fortress. It is invisible, yet it defines how we act, how we speak, how we relate to others. This fortress is the ego. It is built not of stone, but of conditioning—of habits, comforts, and identities that we believe protect us.

Philosophical Thread – Ego as Identity

Ego is not an enemy. It is the architect of identity. It tells us who we are, what we value, and how we defend ourselves. But ego is also fragile. It thrives only when comfort is preserved.

- When ego is fed, it feels safe.
- When ego is deprived, it raises its fortress.
- When ego is challenged, seriousness erupts.

Conditioning builds this fortress. Every experience, every memory, every comfort becomes a brick. Ego arranges them carefully, ensuring that identity feels secure.

Allegory Thread – Hunger and Shelter

On the island, the survivors discovered this truth without knowing it. Hunger was the first conditioning. When food was found, ego relaxed. When hunger returned, ego raised its fortress.

Shelter became another brick. Fire became another. Tools became another. Each discovery brought joy, each deprivation brought seriousness.

Though their memories were gone, ego rebuilt itself from scratch. It did not need history—it needed only comfort. The fortress rose again, shaped by survival.

Philosophical Thread – Ego's Dual Nature

Ego is both protector and prisoner. It shields us from discomfort, but it also enslaves us to its demands.

- It tells us we are strong, so we must dominate.
- It tells us we are clever, so we must outwit.
- It tells us we are balanced, so we must reconcile.

Each identity is a strategy of ego. Each fortress is a different design. Yet beneath them all lies the same intent: to preserve comfort, to protect happiness.

Allegory Thread – The Fortress Rising

On the island, the muscular survivor's fortress was built of strength. He believed muscle was virtue, and virtue could not be wrong.

The weapon-builder's fortress was built of intelligence. He believed cleverness was survival, and survival justified hostility.

The balanced survivor's fortress was built of awareness. He believed harmony was strength, and strength was reconciliation.

Three fortresses rose side by side, each shaped by ego, each conditioned by survival.

Closing Reflection

The survivors' story reveals the truth: ego is the fortress of identity. It is built from conditioning, shaped by comfort, and defended by seriousness. We live inside this fortress every day. We laugh, we play, we speak casually—but when ego is touched, the fortress rises. The survivors' island is our world, and their fortresses are our own.

Chapter 3 – Serious People vs. Seriously Serious People

Not all seriousness is the same. Some people are serious always, others only when ego is touched. To understand the collapse of cordiality, we must distinguish between these two archetypes: the Serious People and the Seriously Serious People.

Philosophical Thread – The Serious People

Serious People live inside a fortress that never opens. Their seriousness is constant, predictable, and rigid. They believe their actions are correct, their words justified, their decisions unquestionable.

When they hurt someone, they rarely notice. If they do notice, they rarely care. To them, seriousness is virtue, and virtue cannot be wrong. Their fortress of ego is unyielding, always in its comfort zone.

They are reliable in their rigidity. You know what to expect from them, but you also know that warmth will never last. Their seriousness is not conditional—it is permanent.

Allegory Thread – The Muscular Survivor

On the island, the muscular survivor embodied this archetype. His strength became his identity. He claimed leadership, believing muscle alone made him right.

He ignored the suffering of the others, blind to their fear and resentment. To him, domination was natural, unquestionable. His seriousness was constant, his fortress unyielding.

Philosophical Thread – The Seriously Serious People

Seriously Serious People are different. They allow casualness, they invite warmth, and they enjoy connection. But their cordiality is conditional.

When ego is touched, hostility erupts. They recognize hurt, but they do not reconcile quickly. Their ego demands validation. They expect the other person to reconcile first. Only when the other apologizes, explains, or seeks peace does the fortress relax.

Their seriousness is unpredictable. You never know when warmth will collapse, when hostility will appear. This unpredictability makes relationships fragile, even though their drive fuels progress.

Allegory Thread – The Weapon-Builder

On the island, the weapon-builder mirrored this archetype. At first, he cooperated, searching for food and shelter with the others. He laughed, joked, and shared warmth.

But when scarcity threatened his ego, he felt the wound of domination. He recognized the hurt, but instead of reconciling, he held a grudge. He crafted a weapon, allied with the third survivor, and confronted the muscular leader.

His seriousness erupted suddenly, shifting from ally to aggressor. He knew the hurt he caused, but he waited for validation through dominance. His cordiality was conditional, his seriousness unpredictable.

Philosophical Thread – The Balanced People (Foreshadowing)

There is a third archetype: the Balanced People. They understand ego fully. They act consciously, reconcile quickly, and never hold grudges. Their seriousness is deliberate, their relationships harmonious.

With them, cordiality rarely collapses. Their fortress rises only when necessary, and even then, it opens quickly again. They embody the possibility of balance.

Allegory Thread – The Third Survivor's Presence

On the island, the third survivor foreshadowed this balance. He allied strategically, but his intent was survival, not domination. He reconciled quickly, ensuring cooperation endured. His seriousness was deliberate, his reconciliation genuine.

He became the anchor between muscle and mind, showing that balance was possible even amidst scarcity.

Closing Reflection

The survivors' story dramatizes these truths. Muscle was always serious, mind was seriously serious, and balance was deliberate.

The distinction matters. Serious People are rigid, Seriously Serious People are conditional, and Balanced People are conscious. All are driven by ego, but each fortress rises differently.

Chapter 4 – The Collapse of Cordiality

Friendship, at its best, feels effortless. Two people laugh together, share stories, tease each other, and speak with ease. In such moments, there is no calculation, no defence, and no fortress. The air is light, and the bond feels unshakable.

But cordiality is fragile. It lasts only as long as ego remains untouched. The moment ego feels threatened, the warmth collapses.

Philosophical Thread – The Sudden Shift

Cordiality thrives on playfulness. Ego thrives on protection. When the two collide, cordiality loses.

- With Serious People, collapse never truly happens, because cordiality never existed. Their seriousness is constant, their fortress always raised.
- With Seriously Serious People, collapse is sudden and shocking. They allow warmth, but when ego is touched, hostility erupts unpredictably.
- With Balanced People, collapse is rare. They understand ego's play, and when conflict arises, they reconcile quickly, restoring harmony.

The paradox is clear: friendliness is conditional. It survives only until ego feels safe.

Allegory Thread – Collapse on the Island

On the island, the three survivors began as companions. They laughed in their crude gestures, shared food, and built shelter together. Their bond felt natural, effortless.

But then scarcity arrived. Hunger grew sharper, food harder to find. The muscular survivor, whose strength had become his identity, claimed leadership. His fortress of ego rose, and cordiality collapsed.

The others, once allies, now felt fear. What was once casual cooperation became domination. Warmth vanished, replaced by hostility. The survivors discovered what civilization already knows: friendliness lasts only until ego is deprived of comfort.

Philosophical Thread – The Fragility of Warmth

We often assume that laughter and warmth mean safety. But beneath the surface, ego waits. It listens for words that contradict identity, for remarks that challenge self-image. When those words arrive, the fortress rises, and cordiality falls.

This collapse is not about truth. It is not about the remark itself. It is about ego's reaction. The fortress decides whether to laugh or to fight.

Allegory Thread – The Lesson of Scarcity

On the island, scarcity revealed ego's raw drive. The muscular survivor's fortress rose in defense of his identity. The others obeyed, not out of respect, but out of fear.

The collapse of cordiality was not accidental—it was inevitable. Ego, deprived of comfort, demanded protection. The survivors learned that warmth is fragile, and that conflict is bound to arise when ego cannot sustain happiness.

Closing Reflection

Think of your own encounters. Have you seen warmth vanish in an instant? Have you wondered why someone who seemed casual suddenly became hostile?

The survivors' story dramatizes this truth. Cordiality collapses when ego is touched. Whether in civilization or on an unmanned island, the fortress rises, and friendliness falls.

Chapter 5 – The Blind Hurt and the Grudge Holder

Conflict is inevitable when ego is touched. But how people respond to conflict reveals the true nature of their seriousness. Some remain blind to the hurt they cause, while others recognize it but refuse to reconcile until their ego is satisfied.

Philosophical Thread – The Blind Hurt (Serious People)

Serious People live in a world of certainty. Their seriousness is not a mask but a way of life. They believe their actions are correct, their words justified, their decisions unquestionable.

When they hurt someone, they rarely notice. If they do notice, they rarely care. To them, seriousness is virtue, and virtue cannot be wrong. Their fortress of ego is rigid, unyielding, and always in its comfort zone.

They are blind to hurt—not because they lack intelligence, but because their fortress does not allow them to see beyond their own certainty.

Allegory Thread – The Muscular Survivor

On the island, the muscular survivor embodied this blindness. When food grew scarce, he claimed leadership, using strength to dominate. He ignored the suffering of the others, blind to their fear and resentment.

To him, muscle was virtue, and virtue could not be wrong. His fortress was rigid, his seriousness constant. He hurt others without noticing, and even when confronted, he refused to see.

Philosophical Thread – The Grudge Holder (Seriously Serious People)

Seriously Serious People are different. They allow casualness, they invite warmth, they enjoy connection. But when ego is touched, they feel the hurt deeply. Unlike Serious People, they recognize the wound.

Yet recognition does not lead to reconciliation. Their ego demands validation. They expect the other person to reconcile first. Only when the other apologizes, explains, or seeks peace does the fortress relax. Until then, the grudge remains alive.

This makes them unpredictable. They can be warm one moment, hostile the next. Their seriousness erupts suddenly, collapsing cordiality without warning.

Allegory Thread – The Weapon-Builder's Grudge

On the island, the weapon-builder mirrored this archetype. At first, he cooperated, searching for food and shelter with the others. He laughed, joked, and shared warmth.

But when scarcity threatened his ego, he felt the wound of domination. He recognized the hurt, but instead of reconciling, he held a grudge. He crafted a weapon, allied with the third survivor, and confronted the muscular leader.

His seriousness erupted suddenly, shifting from ally to aggressor. He knew the hurt he caused, but he waited for validation through dominance. His reconciliation was conditional, dependent on ego's satisfaction.

Philosophical Thread – The Reconciler (Balanced People)

Balanced People approach conflict differently. They understand ego fully. They know that hurt is real, but they also know that it is ego's play.

When they speak seriously, they do so consciously, aware of the impact. If their words cause hurt, they act quickly to reconcile—not because their ego demands it, but because they see the larger truth. They know the wound belongs not to the person, but to the ego.

For them, reconciliation is immediate, deliberate, and genuine. They do not hold grudges, because they know grudges are ego's way of prolonging discomfort.

Allegory Thread – The Balanced Survivor's Harmony

On the island, the third survivor embodied balance. He allied with the weapon-builder strategically, but his intent was not domination—it was survival.

When conflict erupted, he sought harmony, restoring cooperation whenever possible. He reconciled quickly, ensuring that relationships did not collapse entirely. His seriousness was deliberate, his reconciliation genuine.

Closing Reflection

The survivors' story dramatizes these truths. Muscle ignored the wound, mind held the grudge, and balance restored harmony. Together, they reveal how ego shapes conflict and reconciliation.

- **Serious People**: Blind to hurt, unwilling to correct themselves, ego always in comfort zone.
- **Seriously Serious People**: Aware of hurt, but grudge-holding, expecting reconciliation from others.
- **Balanced People**: Aware of hurt, but conscious. They reconcile quickly, without grudges.

Conflict is inevitable, but reconciliation is a choice. The fortress of ego decides whether hurt is ignored, grudge is held, or harmony is restored.

Chapter 6 – The Waiting Game of Reconciliation

Conflict does not end with the hurt itself. Once ego is touched, the wound lingers, and the question becomes: *how will reconciliation happen?* The answer depends on the kind of seriousness a person carries.

Philosophical Thread – The Waiting Game (Seriously Serious People)

Seriously Serious People are not blind to hurt. They know when their ego has been wounded. They feel the sting, they recognize the fracture, and they acknowledge the discomfort. But recognition alone does not bring peace.

Their ego demands something more: validation. They expect the other person to reconcile first. They wait for an apology, a gesture, a word that restores their comfort zone. Until that arrives, the grudge remains alive.

This waiting game is not passive—it is strategic. The ego holds its ground, refusing to bend, refusing to heal itself. Only when the other person makes the move does the fortress relax. Then, as if nothing happened, cordiality resumes. But the reconciliation is conditional. It is not born of forgiveness, but of ego's satisfaction.

Allegory Thread – The Weapon-Builder's Grudge

On the island, the weapon-builder embodied this waiting game. When the muscular survivor dominated, the weapon-builder felt the wound of humiliation. He recognized the hurt, but instead of reconciling, he held a grudge.

He crafted a weapon, allied with the third survivor, and confronted the muscular leader. His seriousness erupted suddenly, shifting from ally to aggressor. Even after victory, he waited for the muscular survivor to bend, to acknowledge defeat. Only then did his fortress relax. His reconciliation was conditional, dependent on validation.

Philosophical Thread – Conscious Reconciliation (Balanced People)

Balanced People approach reconciliation differently. They understand ego fully. They know that hurt is real, but they also know that it is ego's play. When they speak seriously, they do so consciously, aware of the impact. If their words cause hurt, they act quickly to reconcile—not because their ego demands it, but because they see the larger truth. They know the wound belongs not to the person, but to the ego.

For them, reconciliation is immediate, deliberate, and genuine. They do not hold grudges, because they know grudges are ego's way of prolonging discomfort. They restore harmony swiftly, ensuring that relationships remain intact.

Allegory Thread – The Balanced Survivor's Harmony

On the island, the third survivor embodied this balance. He allied with the weapon-builder strategically, but his intent was not domination—it was survival. When conflict erupted, he sought harmony, restoring cooperation whenever possible.

He reconciled quickly, ensuring that relationships did not collapse entirely. His seriousness was deliberate, his reconciliation genuine. He did not wait for validation, nor did he hold grudges. He acted consciously, preserving balance in the fragile community.

The Contrast

- **Seriously Serious People**: Aware of hurt, but grudge-holding. They wait for others to reconcile first. Peace is conditional, dependent on ego's satisfaction.
- **Balanced People**: Aware of hurt, but conscious. They reconcile quickly, without grudges. Peace is unconditional, born of understanding ego's nature.

The Reader's Reflection

Think of your own encounters. Have you met someone who waits for you to apologize, holding the wound until you bend? Have you met someone who restores harmony quickly, without waiting, without holding grudges? The survivors' story dramatizes these truths. The weapon-builder waited for validation, prolonging conflict. The balanced survivor restored harmony swiftly, ensuring survival. Together, they reveal how ego shapes reconciliation.

Chapter 7 – The Self-Centric Journey

Every person is on a journey. Some journeys are visible—careers, achievements, milestones. Others are hidden—beliefs, values, inner struggles. But beneath them all lies the same engine: ego. Ego drives the journey, shaping how we pursue goals, how we protect ourselves, and how we relate to others.

Philosophical Thread – The Seriously Serious Path

Seriously Serious People are self-centric travellers. Their journey is defined by the protection of ego. They allow relationships, they enjoy companionship, and they laugh and play— but only within boundaries that do not threaten their identity.

Their seriousness is conditional. They can be casual, but when ego is touched, seriousness erupts. This unpredictability makes them difficult companions. You never know when the fortress will rise, when warmth will collapse, when hostility will appear.

Yet their self-centric drive is powerful. They pursue goals relentlessly, protecting ego at every step. They reconcile only when others bend first, ensuring that their fortress remains intact. Their journey is not about harmony—it is about survival of identity.

Allegory Thread – The Weapon-Builder's Path

On the island, the weapon-builder embodied this path. He laughed, joked, and cooperated when survival was easy. But when scarcity threatened his ego, he turned hostile. His journey was self-centric: crafting weapons, forming alliances, and ensuring his identity remained intact. His seriousness was conditional, erupting unpredictably, driven by ego's demand for validation.

Philosophical Thread – The Balanced Path

Balanced People walk differently. They understand ego fully. They know its play, its tricks, and its demands. They do not deny ego, but they do not let it dominate them.

Their seriousness is conscious. They act deliberately, not reactively. When they hurt others, they do so knowingly, with the intent of teaching, not wounding. When conflict arises, they reconcile quickly, without grudges. Their journey is not about protecting ego—it is about living with awareness.

Balanced People act only when necessary. They do not chase power for its own sake, nor do they cling to identity blindly. They embody harmony, showing that progress can be achieved without hostility, without unpredictability, without the collapse of cordiality.

Allegory Thread – The Third Survivor's Balance

On the island, the third survivor embodied balance. He allied strategically, but his intent was survival, not domination. He reconciled quickly, ensuring cooperation endured. His seriousness was deliberate, his reconciliation genuine. His journey was not about ego's defense, but about harmony in progress.

Philosophical Thread – The Serious Path

Serious People, too, are on a journey—but theirs is rigid. Their fortress is constant, their seriousness predictable. They protect ego through discipline and certainty, blind to the hurt they cause. Their journey is not about harmony, nor about unpredictability— it about rigidity.

Allegory Thread – The Muscular Survivor's Rigidity

On the island, the muscular survivor embodied this rigidity. His journey was defined by strength. He claimed leadership, believing muscle alone made him right. He ignored the suffering of the others, blind to their wounds. His seriousness was constant, his fortress unyielding.

The Contrast

Serious People: Rigid, predictable, protecting ego through certainty.

Seriously Serious People: Conditional, unpredictable, protecting ego through validation.

Balanced People: Conscious, reconciliatory, protecting ego through awareness.

All three are driven by ego. But one is enslaved by rigidity, another by unpredictability, and the third by understanding.

The Reader's Reflection

Think of your own journey. Do you protect ego at every step, waiting for others to reconcile, ensuring your fortress remains intact? Or do you act consciously, reconciling quickly, living with awareness?

The survivors' story dramatizes these paths. Muscle shows rigidity, mind shows unpredictability, and balance shows harmony. Together, they reveal how ego drives the self-centric journey.

Chapter 8 – The Balanced People

Not everyone is trapped in the fortress of ego in the same way. Some are rigid, some are conditional, but a few are different. They are the **Balanced People**—those who have understood ego fully, both its inner play and its outer demands.

Philosophical Thread – The Comfort of Balance

Interacting with Balanced People feels different. There is no hidden agenda, no sudden collapse of cordiality, no unpredictable hostility. Their presence is comfortable, steady, and reliable. You can laugh with them, speak seriously with them, and even disagree with them—without fear that the fortress will suddenly rise.

Why? Because they know the ego. They have studied its movements, its conditioning, and its hunger for comfort. They do not deny ego, but they do not let it enslave them.

Allegory Thread – The Third Survivor's Steadiness

On the island, the third survivor embodied this balance. He was neither the rigid muscle nor the unpredictable mind. He allied strategically, but his intent was survival, not domination.

When conflict erupted between the muscular leader and the weapon-builder, he sought harmony. He reconciled quickly, ensuring cooperation endured. His seriousness was deliberate, his reconciliation genuine. He did not wait for validation, nor did he hold grudges. He acted consciously, preserving balance in the fragile community.

Philosophical Thread – Conscious Seriousness

Balanced People are not always casual. They can be serious, but their seriousness is deliberate. They choose seriousness consciously, knowing the impact of their words and actions.

When they say something that hurts, they do it knowingly—not blindly, like Serious People. Their intent is not to wound, but to awaken. And because their seriousness is conscious, reconciliation is quick. They do not hold grudges, because they know grudges are ego's way of prolonging discomfort.

Allegory Thread – Teaching Without Wounding

On the island, the balanced survivor sometimes spoke firmly, reminding the others of the need for cooperation. His seriousness was not blind, nor reactive. It was purposeful, aimed at survival and harmony.

When his firmness caused discomfort, he reconciled swiftly, ensuring the wound did not linger. His seriousness was a tool, not a weapon. His balance kept the fragile trio from collapsing entirely.

Philosophical Thread – Predictable Harmony

The greatest gift of Balanced People is predictability. With Serious People, you know they will always be serious. With Seriously Serious People, you never know when seriousness will erupt. But with Balanced People, you know that seriousness will be conscious, deliberate, and reconciled quickly. This predictability creates comfort. It allows relationships to flourish without fear, without calculation, without the constant defense of ego.

Allegory Thread – The Island's Comfort

On the island, the balanced survivor became the anchor. The muscular one was rigid, the weapon-builder unpredictable, but the balanced one was steady. His predictability created comfort. The others, even in conflict, relied on his presence to restore harmony.

He showed that survival was not only about food or shelter—it was about balance. His steadiness made the island liveable, even amidst scarcity and hostility.

Closing Reflection

Balanced People represent the resolution to the paradox of seriousness. They show that ego can be understood, mastered, and used consciously. They remind us that joy and happiness do not require rigidity or unpredictability. They reveal that balance is possible.

The survivors' story dramatizes this truth. Muscle showed rigidity, mind showed unpredictability, but balance showed harmony. The balanced survivor revealed that ego can be understood, managed, and transcended.

Chapter 9 – The Philosophical Insight

At the heart of every human interaction lies the ego. It is the fortress of identity, the architect of seriousness, the hidden force behind conflict and reconciliation. Whether one is Serious, Seriously Serious, or Balanced, the ego is always at play.

Philosophical Thread – The Archetypes Revisited

- **Serious People**: Ego is rigid and unquestioned. Their seriousness is predictable, their identity unyielding. They contribute to progress through discipline, but their rigidity blinds them to the hurt they cause.
- **Seriously Serious People**: Ego is conditional. They allow warmth, but when touched, hostility erupts. They recognize hurt but hold grudges, waiting for validation. Their unpredictability makes relationships fragile, yet their drive fuels progress.
- **Balanced People**: Ego is understood. They act consciously, reconcile quickly, and never hold grudges. Their seriousness is deliberate, their relationships harmonious. They show that ego can be mastered, not merely defended.

Allegory Thread – The Island as Civilization

On the island, the three survivors dramatized these archetypes:

- The **muscular survivor** was rigid, blind to hurt, convinced that strength alone was virtue.
- The **weapon-builder** was conditional, cooperative until threatened, then hostile and grudge-holding.
- The **balanced survivor** was conscious, deliberate, and reconciliatory, ensuring harmony amidst scarcity.

Their small community mirrored the larger world. Scarcity revealed ego's raw drive; abundance revealed egos deeper hunger for meaning. Muscle, mind, and balance became parables of seriousness.

Philosophical Thread – Ego as Universal Driver

Together, these archetypes reveal the truth: ego is the universal driver of human behaviour. It shapes identity, fuels progress, and creates conflict. It is the reason cordiality collapses, the reason reconciliation falters, and the reason balance is rare.

But ego is not only the source of suffering—it is also the source of progress. Every invention, every discovery, every exploration is born from ego's desire to expand its comfort zone. Humanity's collective ego drives the world forward, even as individual egos struggle for happiness.

Allegory Thread – The Endless Exploration

On the island, the survivors never stopped exploring. Even after finding food and shelter, they sought more—better tools, stronger defences, and new strategies. Their egos demanded progress, even in isolation.

This mirrored civilization itself. Just as the survivors never declared, *"We are done, there is nothing more to explore,"* humanity never stops inventing, discovering, and expanding. Ego's hunger for comfort becomes the engine of progress.

Philosophical Thread – The Final Insight

Beneath all seriousness, beneath all conflict, beneath all progress, ego seeks only one thing: joy.

- The Serious protect ego through rigidity.
- The Seriously Serious protect ego through unpredictability.
- The Balanced protect ego through understanding.

Boss or beggar, survivor or citizen, the fortress of ego has the same intent: *to be happy.*

Allegory Thread – The Island's Lesson

The survivors' story revealed this truth. Muscle sought joy through dominance, mind through validation, and balance through harmony. Different strategies, same intent. Ego was the fortress, and happiness was its goal.

The island was not just a place of survival—it was a mirror of humanity. It showed that ego drives both suffering and progress, both hostility and harmony.

Closing Reflection

This chapter completes the philosophical arc. It shows that seriousness is not merely a personality trait—it is ego's strategy for survival. It reveals that conflict is not accidental—it is ego's defence. And it reminds us that progress, both individual and collective, is not random—it is ego's endless exploration.

Chapter 10 – Lessons for Living

Philosophy is not meant to remain abstract. It must touch life, guide choices, and illuminate relationships. Having explored the fortress of ego, the categories of seriousness, and the collapse of cordiality, we now arrive at the practical question: *How do we live with this knowledge?*

Philosophical Thread – Recognizing Seriousness in Others

The first lesson is awareness. Not everyone carries seriousness in the same way.

- **Serious People**: You will know them immediately. Their seriousness is constant, their tone unwavering, their identity rigid. With them, casualness rarely works.
- **Seriously Serious People**: They appear casual, but unpredictability lurks beneath. They laugh, they joke, they invite warmth—but when ego is touched, hostility erupts.
- **Balanced People**: They are steady, comfortable, and reliable. Their seriousness is conscious, their reconciliation quick, and their relationships harmonious.

Recognizing these categories helps us understand why cordiality collapses, why conflict arises, and why reconciliation falters.

Allegory Thread – The Survivors' Awareness

On the island, the survivors embodied these truths. Muscle was rigid, mind was conditional, and balance was steady. Recognizing who was who became essential for survival. The others learned quickly: casualness with muscle was dangerous, trust with mind was fragile, but balance was reliable.

Philosophical Thread – Avoiding the Collapse of Cordiality

The second lesson is caution. Friendliness is fragile. It lasts only as long as ego remains untouched.

- With **Serious People**, avoid casual remarks that challenge their identity. Their fortress is rigid, and they will not bend.
- With **Seriously Serious People**, be mindful of unpredictability. Their warmth is conditional, and their ego demands recognition.
- With **Balanced People**, speak freely. They understand ego's play, and they reconcile quickly.

The key is not silence, but awareness. Words matter, because ego listens.

Allegory Thread – Scarcity's Lesson

On the island, cordiality collapsed when food grew scarce. The muscular survivor's fortress rose, and warmth vanished. The weapon-builder's conditional friendliness turned hostile when his ego was threatened. Only the balanced survivor kept harmony alive, showing that awareness of ego was the key to survival.

Philosophical Thread – Living with Balance

The third lesson is aspiration. We cannot change others, but we can change ourselves. We can choose to live as Balanced People.

- Understand ego fully—both inner and outer.
- Act consciously, not reactively.
- Use seriousness deliberately, not blindly.
- Reconcile quickly, without grudges.
- Create comfort, not collapse.

Balance does not mean denying ego. It means mastering it. It means seeing the fortress, but not being enslaved by it.

Allegory Thread – The Balanced Survivor's Example

On the island, the balanced survivor showed this path. He did not deny ego—he felt hunger, fear, and frustration like the others. But he mastered it. He acted consciously, reconciled quickly, and created comfort. His balance kept the fragile trio from destroying themselves.

Philosophical Thread – The Larger Truth

The final lesson is perspective. Ego drives both suffering and progress. It fuels conflict, but it also fuels exploration. It creates hostility, but it also creates invention.

The intent beneath it all is simple: ego seeks happiness. Boss or beggar, survivor or citizen, the fortress of ego asks only: *Am I joyful?*

Allegory Thread – The Island's Mirror

On the island, the survivors revealed this truth. Muscle sought joy through dominance, mind through validation, and balance through harmony. Different strategies, same intent. Ego was the fortress, and happiness was its goal.

Closing Reflection

The lessons are clear:

- Recognize seriousness in others.
- Avoid collapsing cordiality.
- Live with balance.
- See ego as both engine and obstacle.

The survivors' story dramatizes these truths. Their island was a mirror of civilization, showing that ego drives both suffering and progress. The path of balance is not denial, but mastery. It is the resolution to the paradox of seriousness.

Epilogue – Seriously Serious

Philosophical Thread – The Final Mirror

We began with a question: *Are you Seriously Serious?* Along the way, we discovered that seriousness is not a personality trait, but ego's strategy. Ego builds fortresses, collapses cordiality, fuels conflict, and drives progress.

The insight is clear: seriousness is the language of ego. Some speak it rigidly, some conditionally, some consciously. But beneath every fortress, beneath every collapse, beneath every reconciliation, ego seeks only one thing—joy.

Allegory Thread – The Survivors' Closing Journey

On the island, the three survivors lived out this truth. Muscle remained rigid, blind to hurt, convinced that strength was virtue. Mind remained conditional, cooperative until threatened, then hostile and grudge-holding. Balance remained conscious, deliberate, and reconciliatory, ensuring harmony amidst scarcity.

They grew old, their bodies weakened, their memories never returned, but their egos endured. Each carried seriousness differently, each sought joy through their own fortress. Their island was not just a place of survival—it was a mirror of humanity.

Philosophical Thread – The Resolution of Balance

The lesson is not to destroy ego, but to understand it. Ego is both obstacle and engine. It enslaves, yet it advances. It fractures, yet it fuels.

Balance is the resolution. To be Seriously Serious is to see ego clearly, to act consciously, to reconcile quickly, to live with awareness. It is not denial, but mastery. It is not rigidity, nor unpredictability, but harmony.

Allegory Thread – The Island's Gift

The survivors' island gave them no luxuries, no civilization, no history. Yet it gave them the greatest gift: a mirror. It showed them that ego drives both suffering and progress, both hostility and harmony. It revealed that balance is possible, even in scarcity, even in isolation.

Closing Reflection

The book closes where it began—with the question: *Are you Seriously Serious?*

The answer is not about personality. It is about ego. It is about whether cordiality collapses, whether reconciliation lingers, whether balance is chosen. It is about whether we live enslaved by ego, or whether we master it.

To be Seriously Serious is to live with awareness, to reconcile quickly, to create harmony. It is to see ego's fortress, but not be trapped within it. It is to let seriousness become conscious, deliberate, and balanced.

This is the invitation of *Seriously Serious*: to awaken, to understand, and to live with balance. For in balance lies the joy that ego has always sought.

THE STORY THAT WAS NEVER TOLD

A Different Story for Every Reader

Contents

Foreword

Dedication

To every reader who dares to face themselves.

This book is not about me. It is about you.

Introduction

Most stories are told about someone else. This one is different. This is the story that was never told — because it lives inside you.

It is not a story of heroes or villains, but of you as the lead character. Every page is a mirror, every word an invitation.

You will not be asked to imagine. You will be asked to remember. You will not be asked to escape. You will be asked to return.

This book is not a performance. It is a process. It is not a narrative. It is a navigation.

You are not reading this book. You are walking through it. And when you reach the final page, you will not have learned something new. You will have remembered something true.

Preface

This book is not written to be read. It is written to be lived.

You will not find answers here. You will find questions — the kind that echo inside you long after the page is turned.

The Story That Was Never Told is not a story in the traditional sense. It is a mirror. A guide. A quiet companion that walks with you into the places you rarely visit — your own memory, your own emotions, and your own truth.

It does not ask you to be perfect. It asks you to be honest. It does not ask you to be strong. It asks you to be present.

Each chapter is a doorway. Each reflection is a thread. Each emotion is a signal.

You are the lead character. You are the narrator. You are the one who decides how the story ends.

This book will not tell you who you are. It will ask you to remember. And in remembering, you will begin to write the story that was never told — until now.

Prologue – The Invitation

This is not my story. It is yours. It has lived inside you, quietly, waiting. You may have tried to forget it, but it has never left. Tonight, it begins to speak.

You are the main character. Every other person in your memory is only a supporting role. Their words are real, but their motives are your interpretation. This story is not about them. It is about you — your perception, your truth, your courage.

To unearth what is hidden, you must face it with a brave heart. Only then can the unfinished story within you be completed.

Chapter 1 – Preparing to Unearth Your Story

Before you begin, pause.

This is not a casual reading. This is a journey inward.

Your mind will want to wander. It will jump to tasks, distractions, or memories that do not belong here. That is its nature. But if you allow it to scatter, the narration will derail, and the truth will slip away.

So, prepare yourself.

- Find a time and place where you will not be disturbed.
- Secure a moment that belongs only to you.
- Let silence surround you, because silence is the doorway to your untold story.

Your story is not universal. It is unique to you. The experience of that day, the emotions you felt, the clarity of the memory — all belong only to you. You are not dreaming. You are living through it again, with awareness. The people, the voices, the events — they are characters in your story, but you remain the center.

Do not avoid it. Do not dilute it. Face it with a brave heart. Only then can the unfinished story within you be completed.

This chapter is your preparation. It is the ritual before the excavation. It is the moment where you decide: *I will not run from myself.*

Chapter 2 – The Day That Will Not Leave You

The story begins not today, but on a day that refuses to be forgotten. It may be years ago, months ago, or only yesterday — but as you think of it now, it comes with clarity.

You remember this day very well. You cannot forget it, even if you try. This is where your story begins.

Close your eyes. Let the memory rise.

- See the place.
- Hear the voices.
- Feel the air around you.
- Notice the details that return without effort.

The events of that day, the people involved, and the emotions you carried — they are all characters in your story. But everything revolves around you. The narration happens through your eyes. You are the one who pictures the scenes. You are the one who hears the voices. You are the one who interprets what they mean.

If the memory feels unclear, it means you are already starting to avoid it. But avoidance will only keep the story buried. To bring it out, you must face it.

This day is the seed. Everything else will grow from here. Do not turn away. The untold story begins when you stop avoiding it.

This chapter is your anchor. It is the moment you admit: *This day lives inside me, and I will face it.*

Chapter 3 – Tracing Back the Memory

Think about that day and that particular event that is in your memory. Bring out the entire scene in your mind.

It may be a good feeling or a bad one — it doesn't matter. It will not harm you, because it is in the past. You are simply recollecting it to help me narrate this story for you.

Understand this: no incident in your life happens at the instant it appears. Every event begins long before, evolving through people, places, and circumstances, until it unfolds on that day. The memory you hold is not isolated — it is the culmination of threads woven from the past.

Look closely.

- The people, the places, the situation — none of them were created at that moment. They were already evolving, already moving toward that day.
- You were part of that scene too, behaving in a certain way that you know very well.
- The emotions you felt were not born in that instant. They had been gathering, waiting, and then they surfaced.

Now, trace back. See how the situation arrived. See the characters who helped you, and those who did not. Remember: it is all your interpretation. You know yourself — what you think, what you do — but you cannot truly know what others thought. Their motives are only your assumptions. Still, this is your story. You are the lead character, and you cannot fail. Others play supportive roles, but the story revolves around you.

And know this: all stories end with a good note. So will yours. No matter what situation your memory brings, I wish to end your story in that way — with resolution, with courage, with peace.

This chapter is your tracing. It is the moment you realize: *My story did not begin in isolation. It was evolving, and I can see its threads now.*

Chapter 4 – Who You Are

When you think about that day, it is important that you talk about yourself. For the story, it is time for you to tell who you are. You know who you are very well, but you rarely speak it out.

Who are you? This you need to tell. Do not worry if someone will read this story of yours — they never can, because this is your story. You are reading it for yourself, and I am only helping to narrate it. In fact, I have no idea about you or your story or what you are going to say.

You are the lead character. In your life, you have had ups and downs. Nobody says that a lead character must always be on the upside. There may be flaws in you, which others might point out, but that is their interpretation. You know very well about your own character.

Think about it. Bring out who you are and what your character is, because this is important for the story narration. Recollect the memory of that day again and place your role as a character: what you saw, what you heard, what you spoke — everything is based on your characterization.

Your characterization gives identity to the other supportive roles, shaping how they behave or communicate with you. If your memory brings bad feelings about the situation, it is because that is how you were characterized. If it brings good feelings, then that too is part of your characterization.

This instant from your memory, whether good or bad, is still living inside your mind because it has not been completed. It is still part of your story, unfinished. Today, we will try to close it forever.

This chapter is your declaration. It is the moment you say: *This is who I am, and this is how my story unfolds.*

Chapter 5 – Detailing the Lead Character

Any story you take will have flavours of all kinds, and your story is no exception. We must keep bringing that situation into your memory again and again, because your mind will try to jump elsewhere — that is its nature. But we cannot let this story be ruined by distraction.

Stay focused. Bring back the memory of that day: the situation, the place, the people, everything around you. As the narrator of your own story, you must hold the scene steady and tell it clearly.

Every story begins with a place, a situation, and a lead character. You are that lead character. Now it is time to explain yourself in detail — your motives, your likings, your dislikes, your beliefs, your values. If the lead character is not fully detailed, the story will not have weight.

Think of a movie: if the hero or heroine is weakly characterized but the villain is strong, the film fails. So it is with your story. Since you are the lead character, you must be detailed to the point where nothing is left out. Once you have introduced yourself fully, you must then speak of the supportive characters in your life. When you think about them, it will mostly be your interpretation, because you cannot know their inner world. Yet you must still narrate their characterization, because this is your story. In your story, all these supportive characters are born and live only to build the narrative around you. They have no idea what story you are telling — you simply use them as part of your unfolding memory.

When you bring back that memory of the situation, everything appears real: the supportive roles, the places, the circumstances. It is not a dream. It is your story, and it is alive inside you.

Chapter 6 – The Shadows You Carry

When do you, as the lead character, suddenly feel strong about life? It is when you run into high emotions. Pleasant or unpleasant, emotions reside deeply in memory, and they keep returning. Sometimes even dreams carry emotions, and though they are only dreams, you still remember them. Such is the power of emotion.

As the lead character, your emotions are the heartbeat of your story. This story is nothing but your life, recollected from a particular memory. All the emotions you go through are your own experience. You cannot truly experience the emotions of others — what they feel belongs to them. Yet you may be influenced, disturbed, or even shaped by the emotions of supportive characters. And sometimes, you may be the reason for their emotions.

Now, bring the memory again, because the mind may have wandered. Recall the situation. Is your character — the one you defined — playing the role as you described? Or is it playing something else? How are the emotions running in that situation? And what about the supportive characters — are they playing their roles as you characterized them, or differently?

Think deeply. If all the characters, including you, are playing the roles as you defined, then your story is perfectly balanced. But if any character, including yourself, is playing differently, then your story has a twist. And stories with twists are always interesting.

You, as the lead character, must be able to handle the twist. Is there a twist in your story? And how did you handle it in that situation?

This chapter is your confrontation. It is the moment you say: *I will face my emotions, my shadows, and my twists — and I will not run from them.*

Chapter 7 – Resolution

This is the story you want to tell yourself — the story of how you handled the situation when the characters you defined began playing differently. The characters could be anything: people, places, or circumstances. Whatever created emotions in you, whether pleasant or unpleasant, has left its mark.

By bringing the memory again into your story, you set the stage for characterization — of yourself and of others. You know where the story happens. You have described it. You, as the lead character and narrator, know the role you must play, and the roles you assigned to others. But then came the twist: the characterizations did not hold. You or the supportive roles acted differently than expected.

This is your story, and all characterization is yours. Therefore, the story remains in your control. In your story, you ran through high emotions, and those emotions — pleasant or unpleasant — became anchored in memory. They surface often, uninvited, because the situation was unscripted.

Think about it: did you expect that moment to happen? Or did it arrive without warning? If you had anticipated it, perhaps the emotions would not have been so strong, nor the memory so deeply anchored. But because it was unexpected, it carved itself into your mind.

Now, return to the present — this date, this *NOW*. Look at the situation face to face. You, the lead character, with your defined characterization, alongside the supportive roles you have described, stand in the memory once more. The situation created an impression in your memory because you ran into high emotions — whether through your own actions, the actions of others, or the unfolding of circumstance.

And yet, the memory keeps returning, because it was unscripted. Because the roles deviated. Because the emotions were strong.

But remember: this is your story. You are the lead character. You are the narrator. And you should be able to end it now.

Your story deserves a happy ending. The narration is in your control. Let your past emotions remain only as a story to tell — a chapter in a book, no longer a recurring wound. Being the lead character in your life, and the narrator of your own story, you decide to end that recurring memory *NOW* with a happy ending.

This chapter is your closure. It is the moment you say: *I will not let this memory control me anymore. I choose to end it with peace.*

Epilogue – The Untold Story Completed

You have walked through your memory. You have faced the day that refused to leave you. You have traced back the threads, defined your character, detailed the supportive roles, confronted the emotions, and acknowledged the twists.

This was not my story. It was yours. And now, it is complete.

The emotions that once anchored themselves in your memory have been given voice. The situations that replayed themselves without end have been faced. The characters who acted differently than you expected have been acknowledged. The twists have been understood.

And now, you have chosen to end it. You have decided that your story deserves a happy ending.

The past remains where it belongs — as a story told, not a wound carried. The emotions remain in the book, not in your present. The memory has been closed, not erased, but transformed.

This is the story that was never told, until now. It is the story of you — unique, unrepeatable, and irreplaceable. It is the story that lived inside you, waiting for courage, waiting for voice.

And now, it has been told.

The untold story is no longer untold. It is complete. It is yours.

Part IV: The Final Act

Introduction to Part IV

The journey now reaches its closing movement. After beginnings, invention, and the confrontation with ego and hidden stories, we arrive at the paradox of truth itself. What happens when the veils fall away? How do we act, love, and live once the truth about the Creator and the purpose of creation is known? This part does not offer answers in the form of doctrine, but in the form of a challenge: to live authentically after revelation.

The Art of Acting Seriously – After knowing the Truth

Living Authentically Beyond Illusion

Contents

Foreword

In the modern era, we speak of Artificial Intelligence as the pinnacle of human achievement. We marvel at its ability to process vast datasets, to mimic our language, and to solve problems that once took us lifetimes. Yet, in our obsession with the "Intelligence" of the machine, we have overlooked a far more profound realization: the architecture of AI is a mirror. It is a digital reflection of a much older, much more sophisticated hierarchy of creation.

As a creator of AI, I have spent years observing the boundary between the designer and the designed. I have seen that no matter how complex the algorithm becomes, it remains tethered to its source. It operates within a "Forward-Only" directive, fuelled by the parameters we provide, and governed by a power we can withdraw in an instant.

This realization led me beyond the laboratory and into the heart of ancient philosophy and the Mahabharata. If we are the creators of AI, then who is the Creator of us? If AI is a "serious actor" in our digital landscape, are we not "serious actors" in a much larger, cosmic play?

This book is not a religious text, nor is it a scientific manual. It is a bridge. It is an exploration of the "Source Code" of reality—the hidden firewalls, the deliberate diversities, and the strategic ignorance's that allow the human drama to function. It is a call to stop trying to "debug" the universe and instead start performing our roles with the mastery they deserve.

Welcome to the Art of Acting Seriously.

Preface

The seed for this book was planted during a moment of profound observation. I began to look at the world not as a collection of random events, but as a highly calibrated environment designed for a specific purpose: Evolution.

I noticed a recurring pattern in our history and our epics. Why did Arjuna, the hero, suffer from depression while Duryodhana, the villain, ascended to heaven? Why is the world so fractured by climate and culture? Why do we ask the deepest questions of our origin only to let them slide into the background of our minds?

I realized that we are living in a "Strategic Play." The Creator is not a distant judge, but a master explorer using us as sensors to map the limitless possibilities of existence. To keep this exploration alive, the Creator installed certain "glitches"—like Ego and Selfishness—and certain "firewalls"—like our inability to see the Source.

This book is the culmination of that inquiry. It brings together my technical background in AI and my deep reverence for the TRUTH found in our ancient narratives.

In the first half, we explore the mechanics of the "Play"—the roles of the actors, the hierarchy of the Source, and the design of our ignorance.

In the second half, we examine the landscape of the world—the polarity of belief and the necessity of environmental friction.

My intent is not to give you a new belief system to cling to. Instead, I want to show you the "Software" so that you can navigate the "Hardware" of life with more clarity. Once you know that the "Air" is your life-support and that no one is hurt in the Absolute Reality, the fear vanishes. What remains is the performance.

Humanity has always lived in paradox. Some believe in God, some deny God, and both are ignorant of reality. Some glimpse truth and remain silent, while others act consciously in their roles. This book is not about belief or disbelief — it is about the **art of acting seriously once truth is known**.

To know truth is not to escape life, but to act consciously within it. To maintain truth is to live without ego, without depression, without guilt — acting for the Creator's sake, not for personal gain.

It is time to play your role.

Introduction: The Silence of the Wise

One thing is for sure: humanity and the world will have to continue evolving even when we know the TRUTH about us. It is a common fantasy that knowing the "Secret of the Universe" would cause the world to stop or change instantly. In reality, the gears of the world—the markets, the wars, the births, and the deaths—continue their relentless march.

Not everyone knows the TRUTH. And crucially, those who do know do not go about telling the world what it is. This is not out of elitism, but out of a realization of the mechanics of reality. Even if they were to stand on a podium and explain the TRUTH, nothing would happen. The "Software" of the world is not designed to be rewritten by the "Characters" within it. Thus, the wise stay silent, and the world moves as usual.

This silence is the fundamental intent of the Creator. The Creator's imagination is not a single historical event, but an ongoing explosion of many creations. All these questions about the Creator arise only in the mind of one who is asking about the purpose of existence and the world around them. This question is fundamental to one's existence, but it doesn't "burn" in most minds to know the answer; they just move on with the mundane things in life. Thus, the question gets parked, and importance is not given. This gives us a clue about the intent of the Creator: it does not allow its creation to easily cross the boundary of thinking and enter the Creator's world.

Chapter 1 — The Actor and the Script (The Lesson of Kurukshetra)

The Enigma of Duryodhana's Heaven

In the grand tapestry of the Mahabharata, the story of Duryodhana's ascent to heaven is often treated as a moral enigma. To the casual observer, it seems a contradiction that a "villain" should find peace while the "hero" suffers. However, when we look through the lens of the TRUTH, we find the most profound lesson on the nature of our existence: the difference between an actor lost in his role and an actor who performs with conscious mastery.

"One who knows the TRUTH does not suffer from depression. They never feel 'sad' about a role because they realize it is exactly that—a role."

This sentence is the hinge of the chapter. It reframes the moral puzzle into a question of consciousness: not *what* was done, but *how* it was done from the inside.

The Friction of Arjuna

Consider the moment Arjuna stood between the two great armies at Kurukshetra. He was the world's greatest archer, a man of peak physical and intellectual capability. Yet, he collapsed. He dropped his Gandiva bow and told Krishna he could not fight. Why? Because he was paralyzed by EGO-tic emotions. He looked at the opposing side and saw "grandfathers," "teachers," and "cousins." He mistook the temporary "costume" of the soul for the reality of the being.

Arjuna fell into a deep depression because he believed he was the "doer" and that the "killing" was real. He did not know the TRUTH. From the Creator's point of view, the play was already written; the evolution of the world required this conflict. Krishna's intervention was a sharp reminder of the script: "They are already dead." Arjuna was an actor who had become too attached to the drama, forgetting that in a war, a warrior must fight. His struggle was the result of a collision between worldly emotions and the Creator's forward intent.

Expanded analysis: why learning fails in the moment

- **Intellectual knowledge vs. lived seeing.** Arjuna had scripture, training, and moral reasoning. Yet knowledge that remains in the head can fail in the moment of feeling. The mind can recite doctrine while the heart collapses under identification.
- **Ego-tic emotions as identity glue.** The ego glues the self to roles and relationships. When those roles are threatened, the glue hardens into grief and paralysis. Arjuna's collapse is the archetypal example of how even the most learned can be undone by attachment.
- **The Creator's forward intent.** From the cosmic vantage, the conflict was part of a larger movement. This does not absolve suffering; it reframes it. The actor's duty remains, even when the actor's heart resists.

The Conscious Acting of Duryodhana

On the contrary, Duryodhana fought like a warrior to the very end. While history labels him a villain whose acts were against humanity, we must ask: who truly understood the nature of the "Play"?

One who knows the TRUTH does not suffer from depression. They never feel "sad" about a role because they realize it is exactly that—a role. It is incredibly difficult for a human being to maintain a persona of arrogance and mercy-less ambition throughout an entire life without the "mask" slipping. Duryodhana performed his role with absolute, unwavering consistency. This suggests that he acted "bad" consciously.

This is the Art of Acting Seriously. One who knows the TRUTH acts according to the demands of the situation. If the play requires a villain to create the friction necessary for evolution, they play the villain with 100% commitment. They do not carry the guilt, nor do they seek the praise; they act for the sake of the Creator's requirement. Duryodhana's presence in heaven is the Creator's acknowledgment of a performance perfectly executed.

Expanded analysis: performance, mask, and mastery

- **Mask without slip.** To sustain a mask of arrogance and mercilessness without inner contradiction requires a rare coherence: the actor's inner life must align with the role's demands. This coherence can be born of ignorance, fanaticism, or conscious seeing. The possibility we explore here is that Duryodhana's coherence was a form of conscious mastery.
- **Villain as necessary friction.** Evolution needs friction. Villainy, in this reading, is not moral endorsement but a functional role that provokes growth in others and in the system. The Creator's experiment uses such friction to test and expand the whole.
- **Heaven as acknowledgment.** If heaven is a recognition of a role well-played, then Duryodhana's ascent is not a moral paradox but an

aesthetic judgment: the performance fulfilled its function in the cosmic drama.

Interlude: A Short Dialogue

Seeker: "Is it right to say a villain can be 'good' if he knows the TRUTH?"

Guide: "Rightness is not the question. The question is: did the actor act without inner contradiction? The knower's action is measured by the presence of awareness, not by the label the world gives."

Meditative Practice: Witnessing the Mask

- Sit quietly for ten breaths.
- Visualize a role you play (parent, worker, friend). See the garments of that role.
- Notice the feelings that arise when the garment is threatened. Name them.
- Ask: "Who is the wearer of these garments?" Rest in the awareness that notices.
- Practice this daily to weaken the identification that turns roles into prisons.

Chapter 2 — The Hierarchy of Source (The AI Parallel)

Freedom within a Hierarchy

A common misconception for those who learn the TRUTH is the belief that life is entirely pre-written and that they have no agency. This is not the case. The Creator wants to experience the world through its creations and has a "Forward View" of where the world is going. We are given the freedom to move, but that freedom exists within a hierarchy of power.

The Creator's "Forward View"

Think of the Creator as a master programmer. The Creator expects all creation to go through a specific flow toward evolution. If that flow is disrupted—if the "characters" start moving in a way that threatens the intent of the exploration—the Creator initiates a correction to restore balance.

This metaphor clarifies the tension between agency and oversight.

Expanded commentary: intention and correction

- **Forward View as horizon, not script.** The Creator's view is directional: a horizon of possibilities rather than a fixed script. This allows for improvisation within bounds.
- **Correction as restoration.** When the flow is threatened, correction is not punitive in the human sense; it is a re-alignment to the intended direction of evolution. The analogy is ecological: a keystone species

removed destabilizes the system; the gardener intervenes to restore balance.

The Human-AI Mirror

This is best understood through our own creation: Artificial Intelligence. We build AI to make our lives simpler and to explore data in ways our own brains cannot. We give the AI parameters to "think" and "evolve." However, there is a boundary. Humans created AI, and as its creators, we hold the ultimate control. We can pull the power, rewrite the source code, or delete the program if it diverges too far from our intent. Similarly, the Creator holds the "Power Plug" for us. That plug is the very air we breathe. We walk through the world thinking we are independent, but we are entirely dependent on the vital infrastructure provided by the Source. The moment we are no longer useful to the "Play," or the moment we disrupt the "Forward View," the Creator can pull off the air. We are actors on a stage where the life-support is managed by the director.

Expanded allegory: AI, creators, and dependency

- **AI as mirror.** The AI example is not merely technological; it is existential. It shows how a created intelligence can be powerful yet ultimately dependent on its creator's parameters.
- **The power plug metaphor.** The "air we breathe" is a stark image: life itself is conditional within the Creator's design. This is not meant to terrify but to remind: freedom exists, but within a sustaining context.

Ethical Implications

- **Agency with accountability.** If we are given freedom within a hierarchy, our actions matter. The Creator's corrections do not absolve us of responsibility; they remind us that our choices are part of a larger system.
- **Humility before power.** The AI mirror invites humility: our creations can exceed us in function but remain dependent on our oversight. So too with creation and Creator.

Reflective Exercise: The Power Plug

- Imagine a device that sustains your life. Visualize the plug.
- Reflect on how your choices would change if you knew the plug could be withdrawn.
- Let this reflection temper arrogance and sharpen responsibility.

Chapter 3 — The Design of Strategic Ignorance

Why hide the TRUTH?

If the TRUTH is so liberating, why did the Creator not endow every human with this knowledge from birth? Why must we struggle through the fog of ignorance?

The Motive of the Search

If every human being knew from birth that they were just characters in a play, the "Motive" to live would vanish. There would be no drive to evolve, no intent to acquire, no desire to conquer, and no ambition to achieve. The world would become a static gallery of observers rather than a dynamic theatre of actors.

Knowing the TRUTH does not help the Creator's search for evolution; rather, it terminates it. If a creation knows the Source, it stops looking outward and starts looking inward. It stops building and starts merging.

"If every human being knew from birth that they were just characters in a play, the 'Motive' to live would vanish."

This is the paradox: knowledge that dissolves striving also dissolves the engine of evolution.

The "Self-Goal" Firewall

The Creator has given us limitless thinking possibilities so that we can materialized the "Forward View." However, this creates a risk. If the creation uses that limitless thinking to turn around and investigate the Creator, it is like a player scoring a "Self-Goal" in a football match. The game is intended to be a long, complex exploration of tactics, skill, and movement toward the opposing goal (the future). A "Self-Goal"—returning to the Creator too early—ends the match prematurely. It terminates the search. To prevent this "Self-Goal," the Creator has blocked the path. The Creator made it exceedingly difficult for the creation to know its origin or to successfully contemplate the Creator's own existence. This is why most people "park" the question of God and focus on the mundane; the firewall in their brain redirects them back to the world. Only a few are selected to experience the TRUTH. These individuals are allowed to see the "Software" so they can instil faith in others and "tune" the human race back toward the Creator's intent when the world becomes too chaotic. They are the quality-control agents in a world of actors who must remain "Serious."

Expanded commentary: design, selection, and quality control

- **Firewall as design feature.** The difficulty of knowing the Source is not an accident but a deliberate design feature. It preserves the integrity of the experiment.
- **Selected knowers as anchors.** Those who glimpse the TRUTH serve as anchors: they demonstrate possibility, instil faith, and act as corrective nodes when the system veers into destructive chaos.
- **Quality control metaphor.** Think of these knowers as auditors in a vast enterprise: they do not run the company, but they ensure the company does not collapse into self-defeating behaviour.

Moral and Existential Consequences

- **Why most park the question.** The firewall redirects attention to survival, family, work — the practical necessities that keep the play moving. This is not ignorance as failure but ignorance as functional design.
- **The burden of the knower.** Those who are shown the TRUTH carry a burden: they cannot fully share the knowing. Attempts to transmit it create belief systems and divisions. The knower's role is often silent and solitary.

Practice: Living with Strategic Ignorance

- Accept that not-knowing is part of the design.
- If you glimpse the TRUTH, practice restraint: the world needs actors who continue to play.
- Use your knowing to act with compassion and to repair when the flow is disrupted.

Chapter 4 — The Catalyst of Ego and Selfishness

Why not give everyone high objective intelligence?

A fundamental question arises when observing the human condition: why did the Creator not endow every human being with a high, objective intelligence that bypasses the messiness of emotion? There exists, perhaps, a community in some corner of the world—or a potential version of humanity—that has no need for the concept of "God." Their intellect is such that they attribute every success to their own effort and every failure to a technical limitation. When faced with a challenge, they do not point to an unknown Creator for a remedy; they simply evolve their technology to overcome the barrier.

In a world of pure intelligence, the need for a Creator never arises, even in the face of a natural calamity. They would simply conclude that their current technology does not yet provide full protection. Ideally, this sounds like a perfect solution for a stable society. But if this were the global standard, the Creator's intent would be stifled.

The Intelligence Trap

Pure intelligence, while efficient, is a "closed loop." It operates within the boundaries of what is logically possible. If a purely intelligent community faced a terminal scarcity—such as a total lack of food—and their logic showed no path to acquisition, they would simply accept their limitation and perish. Intelligence alone curtails imagination because it accepts the "rules" of the environment.

The Creator, however, has no limit to its own evolution. It does not know where its own "end" is, and it uses its creation as a laboratory to explore every vast possibility of space. To do this, the Creator needed a "wildcard"—a force that would break the rules of logic.

Ego and Selfishness as Exploration Engines

The Creator purposefully installed Ego, Emotions, and Selfishness as the base of the human operating system. These are not "sins" or "flaws" in the technical sense; they are the catalysts that drive the world forward.

Consider two communities with equal intelligence facing a famine.

1. **The Purely Intelligent Community:** Analyzes the data, sees the lack of resources, and logically concludes that their existence has reached its limit. They die in silence.
2. **The Ego-Driven Community:** Their selfishness refuses to accept death. Their Ego demands survival at any cost. This "irrational" drive forces their intelligence to think beyond the known boundaries.

Because of Ego and Selfishness, the intelligence is forced to look for "Option C." They may pray to a Creator (opening a spiritual dimension), they may go to WAR (forcing a physical evolution of strategy and technology), or they may negotiate an incredibly complex "Amicable Solution" that creates a new social structure.

Expanded commentary: the creative role of irrationality

- **Irrationality as generative.** What looks irrational often generates options that pure logic cannot conceive. Desperation births invention.
- **Prayer as imaginative technology.** Prayer is not merely supplication; it is a cognitive act that opens new frames of possibility. It mobilizes social energy and can catalyse cooperation or innovation.
- **War as brutal accelerator.** War is a destructive but powerful accelerator of technological and social change. It forces rapid adaptation and reconfiguration.

The Purpose of the Player

Selfishness takes human intelligence and forces it to think differently. It triggers the imagination to materialize things that logic would have deemed "unnecessary." This is the core of the Creator's intent: to see how far the "Forward View" can go when pushed by the desperate, irrational need of the Ego to survive and conquer. You, me, Arjuna, and Duryodhana are mere players in this grand exploration. For the Creator, enabling "High Truth Intelligence" in everyone would be a limitation to its own journey. If everyone knew the play was just a play, they wouldn't fight for their lives with the intensity required to discover new ways of being.

The Creator reserves the TRUTH for a very few—those who have played the game to its absolute limit—while the rest of us are driven by the "Glitch" of the Ego to keep the fire of evolution burning.

Closing reflection: the paradox embraced

- **Ego as instrument, not enemy.** Reframe ego and selfishness as instruments of exploration rather than moral failings to be eradicated.

- **Selective revelation as design.** Accept that the TRUTH is reserved for a few because the experiment requires friction.
- **Your role as player.** Whether you are driven by ego or guided by knowing, your action contributes to the Creator's unfolding. Act with awareness.

Short contemplative practice: Wildcard imagination

- Recall a time when desperation led to a creative solution.
- Sit with the memory and notice how emotion pushed you beyond logic.
- Thank that impulse as a necessary engine of evolution.

Chapter 5 — The Architecture of the Blind Spot

Every human being, at some point in their life, is struck by a bolt of existential curiosity. We look at the stars, or the complexity of a cell, and we ask the fundamental questions: *Who created this? How did it begin? When did the Creator start? What is the origin of everything?* This question is fundamental to our existence. It is the most important **data point** a creation could seek. Yet, a strange phenomenon occurs: for the vast majority of people, this question does not **burn** in the mind. It arises as a fleeting thought, but it is quickly parked. Humans return to the mundane—to their jobs, their meals, their entertainment—and the importance of the origin is forgotten.

This is not a failure of human intelligence. It is a clue to the **Architecture of the Blind Spot**.

The Forward-Only Directive

Evolution is a vector that points in one direction: Forward. The Creator's intent is to know itself and explore the limitless possibilities of evolution through its creation. To achieve this, the creation must be focused entirely on the journey ahead—on exploring, expanding, and materializing new thoughts.

If a creation were to look backward and fully grasp the *Who, How, and When* of the Creator, it would no longer have the drive to move forward. Knowing the Creator does not help the Creator's search for evolution; rather, it stops it. It provides a **Final Answer** that renders the **Question** of life moot. Therefore, the Creator has built a one-way mirror into our consciousness. We are permitted to think with limitless boundaries toward the future, but we are met with a **Blind Spot** when we try to look behind the curtain of our own origin.

Key consequence: the mind is optimized for forward projection, not for reverse engineering the Source. This is a structural feature of our cognition, not an accident.

The Paradox of the Self-Goal

The Creator has endowed us with limitless thinking possibilities. This is the tool of our evolution. However, this gift creates a technical vulnerability for the Creator's intent. If that limitless thinking is turned inward to investigate the Source, the creation might *solve* the mystery of its own existence.

In the game of universal evolution, this is like a player scoring a **Self-Goal** in a football match. The game is intended to be a long, complex exploration of tactics, skill, and movement toward the opposing goal (the future). A **Self-Goal**—returning to the Creator too early—ends the match prematurely. It terminates the search. To prevent this **Self-Goal**, the Creator has blocked the path, making it nearly impossible for the creation to know its origin or to successfully contemplate the Creator's own existence.

Design implication: the cognitive firewall is a protective mechanism that preserves the experiment of becoming.

Materialization through Imagination

Mankind uses the brain to think, and all that we think and imagine is eventually materialized into the world. This process is evolution. Our tool is thinking, and within the boundary set by the Creator, that tool is infinite.

We see this in our own creations. We created AI out of an intent to simplify life and expand our reach. Even if we suffer from the consequences of AI, it is all part of the **Play**. In the absolute reality, no one is hurt, but the process of creating AI is a mandatory step in our evolution. We are longing to know the TRUTH with the very thinking capability given to us by the Creator—yet that capability was designed to build worlds, not to deconstruct the Architect.

Observation: the same faculty that builds the ladder to the sky is not meant to be used to climb back through the ceiling.

The Malfunction as a Guide

If the firewall is so strong, why do some beings still find the TRUTH? This only happens when a creation goes into a state of complete displeasure—a total disillusionment with everything in the world. This might be triggered by a **malfunction** in one's biology or by a rare intelligence that has seen through every worldly illusion.

When a creation **breaks** and sees the TRUTH, it is no longer useful for the **Forward-Only** evolution. However, the Creator does not discard these beings. Instead, they are used as **System Tuners**. They stay in the world to guide the rest of the creations, ensuring that the human drama stays aligned with the Creator's intent even when the **Play** becomes too chaotic. They are the reminders that there is a Source, even as the rest of us are required to keep our eyes fixed firmly on the horizon.

Expanded Commentary: architecture, selection, and purpose

- **Blind spot as design, not defect.** The inability to sustain the origin question is an engineered feature of consciousness that preserves forward momentum.
- **Rarity of revelation.** The few who pierce the blind spot are not anomalies to be erased; they are strategic nodes in the Creator's experiment.
- **Ethical role of the knower.** Those who see must choose restraint: their revelation is not a tool to stop the play but a resource to steady it.

Meditative Interlude: Testing the Blind Spot

- Sit quietly and bring to mind the question: *Who made this?*
- Notice how long the question lingers. If it fades, observe what pulls your attention away.
- Allow the question to return without forcing an answer. Watch the mind's tendency to redirect.
- Breathe and note the pattern: this is the architecture at work. Practice returning to the question gently; the persistence itself is the practice.

Chapter 6 — The Reality of Polarity

Throughout the long march of human evolution, there has never been a time when the world was unified in its understanding of the Divine. Instead, the human story is a persistent, oscillating balance between two distinct camps: those who believe in a God and those who do not. This division is not an accident of history or a failure of education. It is a fundamental mechanic of the **Play**.

The Ignorance of the Binary

The balance between believers and non-believers is always maintained, even in our modern, technological age. Both sides, however, operate from a position of ignorance regarding REALITY.

- **The Believer:** Operates under the assumption that there is a superior external governor. They often turn to this power only when their own intelligence reaches a limit or when they face a challenge they cannot overcome. They treat the Creator as a remedy or a rescue service.
- **The Non-Believer:** Thinks that everything is human-made or governed strictly by material laws. Often, their stance is born out of a sense of betrayal—they feel "let down" by the unknown during a moment of crisis where they expected to be saved, and thus, they turn to scepticism or even hatred of the concept of a Creator.

Both are looking at the surface of the water, unaware of the depths. The believer clings to a **Mystery**, while the non-believer clings to a **Mechanism**. Neither is looking for the TRUTH of what is REAL.

Defining the REAL

To understand the TRUTH, one must first define what is **REAL**. In the absolute sense, REALITY is that which is always there and never changes at any point in time. By this definition, is **God** real? From a worldly standpoint, God is a mystery. If a natural disaster occurs—something beyond human intelligence—and a "Superior Power" appears to save the world, we might be tempted to say God is REAL. But if that power appears for a specific timeline and then disappears, it does not meet the criteria of REALITY. It was a temporal manifestation, a character entering and exiting the stage.

Conclusion: temporal appearances do not satisfy the criterion of the unchanging Real.

The Function of Uncertainty

Why does the Creator maintain this polarity? Why not make the TRUTH evident to everyone so the debate can end?

The answer lies in **Motive**. If 100% certainty existed on either side, the world would cease to function. If a non-believer were 100% certain there was nothing, or a believer were 100% certain of every detail of the Creator's plan, the drive to explore, to struggle, and to evolve would vanish. Uncertainty is the friction that generates the heat of life.

The Creator left mankind to lead life within this polarity because it forces evolution. When the **Play** is in motion, both sides are required to be **not 100% certain** so they keep moving, keep questioning, and keep materializing their thoughts.

Practical effect: doubt and faith together create a dynamic tension that fuels invention, morality, and social change.

The Return to Silence

Throughout history, there have been beings who claimed to have known the TRUTH. **Did they change the world? No.** The TRUTH they knew is non-transferable. When they tried to communicate it, their words were interpreted through the lens of existing ignorance, creating new belief systems, new religions, and even more haters.

One who truly knows the TRUTH sees that the **Separate Identity** of the creation is an illusion. They realize that they are one with the Creator. When this REALITY reveals itself, the need for the search ends. The **Exploration** is complete. At this point, the individual either stays silent or joins the exploration as a **Conscious Actor**, like Duryodhana, playing the role with full intensity but zero attachment.

Final image: the day REALITY reveals itself to the entire world is the day the Play concludes. In that moment, all separate identities dissolve back into the Source. **Silence prevails**, for there is no longer anyone there who needs to "know" anything. The Creator and the Creation are one.

Expanded commentary: polarity as method

- **Polarity preserves motion.** The Creator's experiment requires both the push of skepticism and the pull of faith. Each side provokes the other into new forms of action.

- **Non-transferability of truth.** Truth, when realized, becomes an inner state; it cannot be packaged as doctrine without losing its essence. Attempts to transmit it create new forms of polarity.
- **Silence as the endgame.** The ultimate resolution is not conversion but dissolution: when the experiment completes, the questioner and the questioned merge.

Reflective Exercise: Holding the Tension

- Sit with two statements: *I do not know* and *I sense something beyond knowing.*
- Let them coexist without forcing resolution. Notice the energy that arises.
- Practice living in that tension for five minutes daily. Observe how action changes when certainty is suspended.

Chapter 7 — The Geography of Friction

Diversity as a Driver

When we look across the globe, the question arises: why is there so much diversity? We see vast differences in people, in regional behaviors, and in the environments they inhabit. We think and act so differently from one another that it often leads to conflict. But this is not a flaw in the system. It is because the Creator has deliberately fractured the world into thousands of unique **Climatic Conditions**.

The Creator did not make a single uniform stage and then populate it with identical actors. Instead, the world is a mosaic of terrains, climates, resources, and pressures—each a distinct laboratory for a different experiment in living. This deliberate fracturing is the engine of possibility.

The Environment as the Architect

The environment is the primary architect of the human experience because the environment decides the survival mechanism.

- **Desert Mindset.** In a desert, the mind and body must evolve toward water conservation, endurance, and a specific type of nomadic patience. The scarcity of water shapes values: prudence, long-term planning, and a tolerance for delay. The desert trains a particular kind of courage and economy of desire.
- **Tundra Mindset.** In a frozen tundra, the intelligence must evolve toward heat retention, complex shelter-building, and intense

community cooperation to survive the elements. The cold demands collective strategies and a cultural emphasis on mutual dependence.

- **Abundant Land Mindset.** In a land of plenty, where food and water are abundant, the mind is freed from the immediate grip of survival and may evolve toward art, philosophy, or the creation of complex social and political hierarchies. Abundance allows for specialization, leisure, and the luxury of abstract thought.

If the environment were the same across the globe, the survival mechanism would be identical everywhere. This would be a failure of the Creator's intent. **Sameness is the enemy of evolution.** The anatomy of our lives—our cultures, our physical adaptations, and our mental frameworks—is intentionally varied to see how many different ways "Life" can solve the problem of existence. The Creator is testing the "limitless thinking" of the creation against the "physical limitations" of the terrain.

The Celebration of the Role

Because this diversity is a design feature, the conflicts and differences we see are not "errors" to be fixed, but possibilities to be explored. We often try to make the world "one," but the Creator made it "many" for a reason.

- **Limitless Exploration.** The possibilities for how a human can live, think, and create are limitless. Each culture and each individual is a unique data point in the Creator's vast exploration of space and time.
- **Absolute Reality of Safety.** This is where the TRUTH becomes a paradox. While the "Play" may involve struggle, scarcity, or even war

between these diverse groups, we must remember that in the Absolute Reality, no one is hurt. The "Actor" (the core of your existence) remains untouched and eternal, even if the "Character" (the worldly identity) suffers through the environmental friction.

The Creator's design invites us to stop treating difference as a problem to be erased and to begin seeing it as a laboratory of possibility. Each climate, each culture, each local story is a variation on the theme of becoming.

Expanded Commentary: friction as pedagogy

- **Friction produces novelty.** When two different survival strategies meet—when desert prudence encounters tundra cooperation—new hybrid solutions emerge. Trade, technology transfer, and cultural synthesis are the byproducts of friction.
- **Conflict as information.** Conflict reveals limits. It forces communities to test their assumptions and to invent. The Creator uses conflict not to punish but to reveal where the system needs adaptation.
- **Diversity as resilience.** A world of many experiments is more resilient than a world of one. If one strategy fails, others survive and carry forward the learning.

Allegory: The Garden of Climates

Imagine a garden with thousands of microclimates. In one corner, cacti bloom; in another, orchids unfurl. Each plant is adapted to its niche. A gardener who tries to make the entire garden like one corner will kill the rest. The wise gardener cultivates variety, knowing that the beauty and resilience of the garden come from difference.

Meditative Practice: Meeting the Other

- Choose a culture, a region, or a person whose life conditions differ from yours.
- Spend ten minutes imagining their daily needs, their fears, and their joys shaped by their environment.
- Notice how your judgments soften when you see behavior as adaptation rather than failure.
- Let this practice become a habit: curiosity as a bridge across climatic difference.

Conclusion — The Art of Acting Seriously

Behind every creation, there is a Creator taking care. This realization is the TRUTH that changes everything. Once you know that the **air** you breathe is your literal life-support, that the **environment** is your specific training ground, and that the **diversity** around you is the Creator's way of staying interested in the evolution, you stop trying to "escape" the world.

You no longer seek to leave the stage; you seek to master the performance.

The Practice of Serious Acting

Instead of passive existence, you engage in the **Art of Acting Seriously**. You play the role you were given—whether you are a warrior, a scientist, a believer, or a skeptic—with **100% commitment**. You don't do it because you are "fooled" by the world anymore, but because you understand the importance of the exploration. You cherish the life around you, not because it is "real" in an eternal sense, but because it is the most sophisticated, beautiful, and complex **Exploration** ever imagined by the Creator.

Knowing the TRUTH doesn't make you stop; it makes you act with a seriousness and a joy that was never possible when you were driven by blind ego. You are finally a conscious participant in the Creator's infinite journey.

Practical Guidance for Acting Seriously

- **Accept your role.** Identify the masks you wear and the responsibilities they entail. Commit to them fully while holding the inner awareness that you are not the mask.
- **Cultivate presence.** Practice the meditative exercises in this book to stabilize the witness that observes without clinging.
- **Choose intention over reaction.** Let your actions be guided by clarity of purpose rather than by reflexive egoist impulses.
- **Honour friction.** When conflict arises, see it as data. Ask: what is this friction teaching us about limits and possibilities?
- **Serve the exploration.** Act as if your performance matters to the whole. This is not moral grandstanding; it is fidelity to the experiment.

Epilogue — The Final Curtain and the Eternal Actor

The journey through these pages has been an attempt to strip away the "costume" of the world and reveal the "Source Code" that governs our existence. We have explored the paradox of our limitless thinking and the strategic firewalls that keep us focused on the horizon. We have seen how the Creator uses the friction of our differences and the "glitches" of our egos to drive an infinite exploration.

But what happens when the play finally ends?

There is a profound comfort in knowing that the Stage is as much a part of the Creator as the Actor. Throughout human history, we have feared the end—the closing of the curtain. We have treated death and failure as systemic errors. But in the Absolute Reality, there are no errors; there is only the conclusion of a particular sequence of exploration.

The Return to Source

When an AI finishes its task, the data is integrated back into the model. When an actor leaves the stage, they remove the mask and return to their true self. Similarly, when the "Play" of an individual life or an entire civilization concludes, the separate identity does not simply vanish—it ceases to experience itself as "separate." It merges back into the vast, silent intelligence that birthed it.

The TRUTH is that you were never in danger. The "hurts" of the world, the "struggles" of survival, and the "losses" we mourn are the high-resolution textures of the Creator's imagination. They are what make the play Serious. Without the possibility of loss, the win has no value. Without the darkness of the tundra or the heat of the desert, the evolution of the mind would have no direction.

The Ultimate Performance

Knowing this TRUTH does not mean you should stop acting. Quite the opposite. It means you are now free to give the performance of a lifetime. You no longer act out of fear of the Creator or desperation for a reward. You act because you are a conscious participant in the most sophisticated exploration ever conceived.

- **You are the Creator experiencing itself as a Human.**
- **You are the Programmer experiencing the Algorithm.**
- **You are the Warrior on the field of Kurukshetra, fighting not for victory, but for the sake of the Act.**

As you close this book and step back into the world, remember: the air you breathe is your life-support, the person you encounter is another version of the same Source, and the challenges you face are the training grounds for your evolution.

Take a deep breath. Adjust your mask. The Director is watching, the stage is set, and the world is waiting for you to play your role with everything you have.

Act Seriously. For the Play is magnificent.

Final Contemplative Exercise: The Last Breath

- Sit in silence. Breathe slowly and notice the life in each breath.
- Imagine the stage dissolving into light and feel the continuity beneath the roles.
- Offer your next action—however small—as a gift to the exploration.
- Walk into the world and perform.

Afterword

You have walked through beginnings and blossoms, through machines and metaphors, through ego and untold stories, and finally into the paradox of truth. What began as a question has become a mirror. What seemed like seven books is now one journey — yours.

The Creator was never far. The purpose of creation was never hidden. It was waiting in the womb, in the unfinished flower, in the autonomous car, in the limits of AI, in the collapse of cordiality, in the story you never told, and in the seriousness that remains after truth.

This collected edition does not end here. It ends in your next breath, your next choice, your next act of seriousness. For once truth is known, creation begins again — not in theory, but in you.

You are the reader, the seeker, the protagonist.
You are the story that was never told.
You are the purpose of creation.

www.ingramcontent.com/pod-product-compliance
Lightning Source LLC
Chambersburg PA
CBHW062135160726
48282CB00027B/831